Tales From The Green Side
Volume 1

A Barstool Short Story
Anthology Series

Johnnie L Gilpen Jr. PA-C NRP
Robert "Bob" Creager NRP

U.S. NAVY FMF CORPSMAN

NEC:8404

Published by 8404 Publishing LLC. (www.8404publishing.com) and johnniegilpen.com.

Library of Congress Cataloging-in-Publication Data
Gilpen, Johnnie L. Jr, 1971 –
Creager, Robert, 1967 –
Tales From The Greenside: Volume # 1/ Johnnie L Gilpen Jr.
Includes bibliographical references.
ISBN 979-8-218-32493-3
Library of Congress Control Number: 2023923279

Cover by Huma Rafeeq at dezinsoultions.net.

The author is grateful for permission to include the following: "The Sailor," written by Al Berry. ©1989

If you are interested in receiving Johnnie's newsletter – *Notes and Scribbles from My Desk*, please sign up for free at https://johnniegilpenjr.substack.com/.

Bimonthly, I'll bring you insights into my personal life and writing habits, with updates on what I am working on, special deals I hear about, and new books by other authors that I am reading.

Also, please follow us on Facebook on my *Johnnie Gilpen Author Page*, *Tales from the Green Side* and *Tales from the Back of the Bus*. I can be found on Instagram, X, and YouTube @pa_author.

Advanced Praise

As a veteran of the U.S. Army, I knew little about the U.S. Navy. Reading Gilpen's stories made me realize how unique life is for those Navy warriors who go to the "Green Side". Yet anyone who has raised their hand to serve in any of the U.S. Armed Forces will recognize the absurdity and hilarity of military life, whether on a post, camp, base, or ship. Veterans of any branch of the U.S. military will enjoy and relate to Johnnie's tales!

War stories tend to be dark and show the pain of military service. But sea stories find the humor of serving in uniform with the United States Navy, especially for those on the "Green Side." Gilpen's pen transports you to a cozy barstool with a pint in hand to listen to the hilarious exploits of Navy Corpsmen and their Marines. Don't miss this book!

What differentiates a "sea story" from a "war story"? Humor, of course. Gilpen's collection of well-written adventures from the "Green Side" of the U.S. Navy will delight veterans and civilians alike. Don't miss the adventure!

Harry L. Whitlock EMT-A

Major, USA (Retired)

Hilarious! The language, illustrations, and characters capture the tone and meaning of being an FMF Corpsman. A terrific read!

Frank Bowersox

Chief Hospital Corpsman (AW/FMF/NAO/NAC), USN (Retired)

Tales from the Green Side is a humorous yet insightful peak behind the curtain of life as a Navy Corpsman with the Marine Corps. The personalities and their stories are compelling, and the illustrations help the imagination bring the tales to life for the reader without similar experiences.

Dennis Healy EMT-P

Detective, NYPD ESU (Retired)

I thoroughly enjoyed reading the book. Anyone who has worked in the green side military medicine can relate to the humor and familiarity of these "no shitter" stories.

Nan Jones

Chief Hospital Corpsman (FMF), USN (Retired)

Tales from the **Green Side** truly captures the bond between Marines and their Doc and especially the jackassery of the young men & women who are serving in our Navy and the Marine Corps who call each other brother and sister with pride.

Russ Folley

Command Master Chief Hospital Corpsman (FMF/SW), USN (Ret.)
II MEF Command Master Chief (2016-2019)

Tales from the **Green Side** is an excellent portrayal of the day to day lives of Navy Corpsmen and Chaplains working alongside their Marine counterparts. This well written book along with cartoon illustrations gives you a birds-eye-view of military life, camaraderie, and trust.

Cathy Houghton

Chief Hospital Corpsman (FMF), USN (Retired)

This book is a boisterous read! It is a compilation of stories that have been handed down from person to person. Some based on real events and some slightly embellished (as all stories are), but all of them highlighting the humor and personal interactions found in military life. As you delve into "Tales from the Green Side," you will encounter relatable stories that will bring a smile to your face and some that will make you laugh out loud. You will absolutely love reading this book.

Ed Weeks

Colonel, USAF (retired)

Tales from the Green Side is a true gem! A fantastic read for veterans and non-veterans alike! The stories and illustrations kept me grinning!

Al Berry

Singer - Song Writer
Sgt, USMC

Tales from the Greenside - I can't say more amazing things about the book. It captured my attention right off the bat, which is hard to do. I don't even like reading. I can't wait for the movie to come out. As a retired E-7, a former 0331 Machine Gunner in the Corps, and a seasoned operator, Tales from the Greenside brought back vivid memories of the time I served with Battalion Landing Team 2/8, 24th Marine Expeditionary Unit Special Operations Capable (MEU-SOC). The Marines' bond with the Navy Corpsman, the camaraderie, and the friendship lasts forever - almost 30 years later, Doc and the Freak are still going strong. Johnnie captured places, details, and marine and navy slang like it was yesterday. I almost feel like I'm reliving the 90s like it was yesterday—a highly recommended read for any past, present, or future Devil Dog or Devil Doc.

Signed ...

Frankie The Freak™

"Operators Gonna Operate"

Stefan Talibasco

Sergeant First Class, USA (Retired)

Great read. Took me back to when I was a Marine Infantry NCO. I've seen Corpsmen do great things on and off the battlefield...... and stupid things, too. Much love and respect to our Corpsmen then and now. Brought back some great memories......Thanks, Johnnie.

David L Bradford

Sergent Major, USMC (Retired)
2nd Marine Division Sergeant Major (2014-2016)

My Brother! For what it's worth from an old war horse, I have thoroughly enjoyed the sea stories you have provided me! I had forgotten what it was like for you boys at HQBN (hilarious). Coffee cups are sacred and preventive medicine is essential to water bulls! I loved it and can't wait for what's to come! Think 2/8!

Mark Hardin

Master Sergent, USMC (Retired)

DISCLAIMER
WARNING

This book was written by a **Sailor** about **Sailors** *and* **Marines** - the language used throughout the book is that of a "SAILOR." We do not intend to offend but rather tell the story the way, well…

This book is written to portray events that may or may not have happened. However, the extent to which they are written and/or captured in drawings is purely the imagination of the author and the illustrator.

Each story is an individual story with its unique narrator. Also, check out **The Barstool Dictionary** on *page 177* for military terms and slang you may not know or understand.

Dedication

I dedicate this book to all the Marines, Sailors, Soldiers, Airmen, Coast Guardsmen, and First Responders I served with, to the ones I have met and shared conversation, meals, and drinks with as well. I also want to commemorate this book to the memory of the 12 Marines, the Corpsman, and the Soldier from Battalion Landing Team 2/8 that we lost on May 10, 1996, during Operation Purple Star, and my friend Lance Corporal Jason Thomas.

That which is remembered is not gone!

Think 2/8!

I want to thank my family, especially my mom, for their continued love and help. Most of all, I want to thank my wife Leslie, whose unwavering commitment and belief in me, pushing me to write when my motivation was non-existent, her hours of reading, correcting, giving advice, and your support of my writing, I could not do it without you. Lastly, I want to thank my brother from another mother, Rob Creager! For over 25 years, we have been more than friends. You have been family. Without your drawing for inspiration – I'm not sure this would have come to fruition! Thank you all.

JG

A Special Thanks to My Family, Especially My Wife, Malinda, for Supporting All My Crazy Ideas.

To An Old Amigo "John Forbus" for His Artistic Contribution to My Cartoons and His Unique Perspective on Life.

To the Sailor and Marines of 2nd Battalion, 2nd Marines, the Inspiration for It All.

To the Man Above for Granting Me the Gift of Doodling.

ROB

Table of Contents

Author's Notes

30th October 2023
Mi La Casa
Alfadale Street
Union City, Oklahoma

Sitting here at my desk tonight finishing the final edits of *Tales from the Green Side Volume #1,* it dawned on me, twenty-something years ago I took off my Navy Uniform for the last time. I traded in my *Johnny Cash's* and *Cracker Jacks* for 5.11 paramedic pants, which have since been retired for Carhartt scrubs. Working as a pediatric emergency medicine Physician Assistant is not that much different from being a Corpsman taking care of Marines – except the kids don't cry as much nor do they eat as many crayons. All joking aside, it's the greatest job I have ever had with the exception of being a Corpsman. The struggle of life and death is just as stressful minus of the risk of being shot – most days.

Over the years I have found many ways to deal with the stress of my chosen profession, some healthy, others not so much. However, during PA school I found my voice. I found I could release stress on a keyboard. Some said I should write a book. This is the answer to that challenge. I started writing as an outlet. The further down the rabbit hole I ran, this crazy idea that my stories could help just more than me developed. Maybe my stories could have a two-fold effect. First, help veterans remember the good, hysterical, and most often stupid moments of military life. Second, my stories, while exaggerated, might provide a different insight for family members and civilians who only seem to hear and/or see the hard and sometimes disturbing aspects of military life. I will be honest; I am not sure it is worthy of being called a book. Still not, but I am proud of the work. All of my beta readers have been more than gracious. Their comments reinforce what I had hoped for, which is expressed in the *Advanced Praise* section. But there was one reader's comment that once I read their email, I knew I had achieved my goal. I asked if I could include them in the book. He told me "My words are your words".

The author - Dr. Tom Billings, M.D., was one of my two Battalion Surgeons when I was assigned to Golf Company, Battalion Landing Team 2/8, 24th Marine Expeditionary Unit – Special Operation Capable (MEU-SOC). He was my first supervising physician. I remember being in the front leaning rest position (pushup position for civilians), as they helped us correct our patient note deficiencies. He is one of the reasons I am where I am today – he encouraged me to pursue my education, and my goals of being an advanced provider. I learned a lot from him and Dr. Shepps. While his words are not specific about the book itself, they capture what the book was intended to do. I hope my words do for you what they did for Dr. Billings.

I would like to introduce you to what I have titled "Reflections of a Battalion Surgeon – 25 years down the road..."

Semper Fi,

Johnnie "Doc" Gilpen

Union City, Oklahoma

Reflections of a Battalion Surgeon –

25 years down the road...

Tom Billings, M.D.
Lieutenant, Medical Corps, USN (1994-1998)
Battalion Surgeon, 2nd Battalion, 8th Marines, 2nd MARDIV

Thanks Johnnie. I do have a few things I have thought about over the years. The first thing that comes to mind is the awesome learning and education that was going on. Some of my favorite memories are of us sitting around a field BAS and some in-service going on. It was so pure, so clean. Our young corpsmen were like sponges, maybe because of the situation and where we were going. But after so many years of educating people, I think of you all like that first hunting dog that happened to be the best one of a lifetime, and I didn't know it at the time. I remember all the other learners, like the ship corpsmen or the army medics, coming to our education too it was because of our corpsman and their attitude.

This dovetails into my second thought. I wasn't the only one that thought you all were special. Each week, when we would have our command meetings, it was amazing to see how much the CO, XO, and the company commanders loved you guys. They were very thankful for your skills and devotion. They would really go to bat for you as well.

The next thing I want to mention is about our corpsman who died in the helo crash – Garman. Not long before the crash, he gave me a pretty fancy cigar from Cuba. He said, "Doc, I would like you to have this." I was a little surprised. I didn't know him well, but I wasn't going to turn down a good cigar. I didn't get a chance to smoke it before he died. I still haven't smoked it. It sits on the wall in my hunting cabin by a Turkey fan. I think of him and you all whenever I walk into the cabin. I remember his mom showed me a letter he wrote her right before the crash. It said something like...

"Mom, I am sitting on the stern of the Saipan. The sun is setting, and as I'm watching it, I realize there is nowhere else I would rather be. This is where I belong."

His mom said thank you to me for helping her son enjoy the last days of his life. But I think this is an example of how great you all were. Corpsman have a very tight, special family, and Garman and his mom were very gracious to talk about it. I am happy to be a very small part of it.

I would also be amiss if I didn't mention all the times you all got me out of trouble. You all taught me to be a better human. And maybe a teenie bit of a leader. I haven't forgotten all the times that a couple of corpsmen picked me up by the arms and led me out of a bad situation. Even getting me home or over the quarter-deck. I will always be grateful, and thanks for letting me give you a few thoughts.

Tom B

Foreword

Geoffrey Chaucer in Jacksonville, NC

In the congratulatory email I sent to Johnnie upon learning that he had been selected as a 2017 Pat Tillman Military Scholar, I wrote: "your words communicated what you needed to say to the audience that needed to hear it." Six years later, in writing *Tales from the Green Side: Volume 1 . . . A Barstool Short Story Anthology*, Johnnie again shares military stories about Marines and Sailors that communicate what needs to be said. This time, however, he writes humor-filled tales for a more heterogeneous audience. Johnnie writes not only to honor the experiences of the service men and women mentioned in the book's dedication, but also to help their civilian friends and families better understand how the experience of military service has and continues to shape their lives.

I first met Johnnie when he was still an emergent writer. I say emergent because he hadn't yet begun writing—or telling—*his* story. I'm not sure he realized he had stories worth telling. Johnnie was in the process of applying for a Pat Tillman Foundation Scholarship and my service on the University of Oklahoma's Pat Tillman Scholarship Committee involved assisting veteran applicants in the process of writing and revising their application essays. The two 400-word essay prompts seemed straightforward, but were actually deceptively complex: the first essay prompt asked applicants to write about their motivation to serve and the most important lesson they learned from their service. The second asked how they planned to serve the greater community upon completing an advanced degree. The key to answering? Deep introspection to uncover authentic answers that bridged past and future service, followed by composing the narrative that told that story.

I read and provided feedback for the two essays Johnnie drafted for his Tillman application. At our first meeting to discuss my suggestions for revision, I explained that what he had written was what he thought the Tillman selection committee wanted to hear. This didn't initially sit well with this man who had more life experiences and publications on his resumé than anyone I'd ever met. I realized that I needed to persuade–no, to convince–Johnnie that his answers needed to tell *his* story. We talked about what I meant by this. At some point, Johnnie realized that my feedback was more than just encouragement–that I was essentially authorizing him to find *his* voice and to write *his* story, and not just because he was applying for a prestigious military scholarship, but rather because his story was a story that needed to be told. To be heard. To be read. To be heeded. To be understood. Johnnie trusted me enough to take these suggestions to heart. He found his voice. He dug deeply, hashed out, and connected the stories of *his* service in another round of Tillman application essay drafts. *His* stories moved me to tears. At our second meeting, he told me that writing them had made him cry.

Johnnie continued to write and to identify as a writer even before learning that he had been selected as a 2017 Tillman Scholar. With the support provided by the Tillman Foundation, he completed OU's Physician Assistant Program and began practicing Pediatric Emergency Medicine at the Children's Hospital of Oklahoma. He also continued writing, publishing, for example, "The Circus is Coming to Town " about working as a medical practitioner during the COVID pandemic, for *The War Horse Journal,* a nonprofit that publishes journalism about military service.

And then, because he wanted to inspire veterans and first responders to find their voices and tell their stories, he started a newsletter on *Substack* called *Notes and Scribbles from My Desk* to publish his story "Why Do We Write . . .". Since, he has founded *8404 Publishing, LLC.* Now, in *Tales from the Green Side: Volume 1 . . .A Barstool Short Story Anthology,* Johnnie has invented a civilian author surrogate named John and his sidekick illustrator named Rob riding from the Midwest to Florida on "the back of [their] Harley's... in search of stories that need telling." John the narrator, a self-described humorist in the tradition of Mark Twain, Will Rogers, and Garrison Keillor, wants "to help others write about anything that they can't put pen to paper themselves . . . to write stories that make people laugh but also remind them of something that was good and meaningful in their lives."

When Johnnie asked me to be a Beta reader for the draft of *Tales from the Green Side,* I immediately consented. Below is my initial response after finishing the book:

> I read the entire *Tales from the Greenside* from start to finish yesterday. Honestly, I couldn't stop reading! Oh, the hilarity! Having lived nearly half of my life in Chicago, I appreciated the Blues Brothers allusion. You're a humorist! Who knew? Not only did I get a bit of Mark Twain in the humor, I also sensed something that you may have not intended. *TGS* reminds me of Geoffrey Chaucer's *Canterbury Tales*! Have you ever read it? A motley crew of pilgrims stop overnight at the Tabard Inn for a break and are challenged by the host to a tale-telling contest.

"The Miller's Tale" is by far one of the bawdiest, irreverent, and hilarious of the bunch... "The Miller's Tale" and "The Wife of Bath's Tale" are often favorites because of their bawdy content. Readers want to laugh until they cry or laugh and cry simultaneously, especially at what seems irreverent, which is what I did reading your book (and Chaucer). So, you're a 21st century Chaucer.

After reading my email, Johnnie wrote back asking if I would be willing to write a forward for the book, mentioning that it could serve as a bridge for civilian readers. He then added, "You know this is all your fault, Doc?" With humility, respect, and awe, I here take up his gauntlet to write about the parallels between Johnnie Gilpen's *Tales from the Green Side* and Geoffrey Chaucer's *Canterbury Tales*.

Chaucer's *Canterbury Tales* begins with a layered frame narrative told from the point of view of a pilgrim also named Chaucer. Johnnie Gilpen's *Tales from the Green Side* starts with a similarly layered frame narrative told by a humorist writer named John. Both works include prologues that introduce the setting and the inspiration for the tales that follow. In the "Prologue" of the

Canterbury Tales, the pilgrim Chaucer explains that the proprietor of the Tabard Inn in Southwark, South London, Harry Bailey, inspires the tales that follow by challenging the twenty-nine pilgrims staying at his inn before journeying to the shrine of Saint Thomas Becket in Canterbury to a tale-telling contest. The winner will receive a free meal at the inn upon their return from the pilgrimage. Harry Bailey's parallel in *Tales from the Green Side* is Jack, and the Tabard Inn becomes Jack's BAS Bar and Grill and the Triangle Inn. Jack, a retired Navy FMF Hospital Corpsman Senior Chief whose younger version is described as "the cartoon character on a box of Crackerjacks," is another of Gilpen's fictional avatars in the book.

John and Rob are pilgrims on a journey in search of stories, or tales, to retell in the book they want to write. The patrons who regularly frequent Jack's BAS Bar and Grill are also pilgrims, as Jack explains, "To an outsider, it's just another bar, but for the Sailors and Marines who walk through those doors, especially my regulars, it's a refuge, a safe harbor from the day-to-day grind of military life, hence the name, BAS ... "Battalion Aid Station." The Bar and Grill is decorated with so much military memorabilia that Rob describes it as a "military history museum," to which Johnnie marvels, "I wonder what the story is with this place." In response to his wonderment Jack offers the following challenge and reward: "If you boys come back in a couple of hours, and every night till you leave, buy the men and women who call this place theirs a few rounds . . . by the time you ride out of town Tuesday . . . if you two do not have enough material to fill at least two books, not only is your tab on the house, I'll cover the bill at Triangle Inn, too!"

Perhaps the most fascinating parallels between *Tales from the Green Side* and the *Canterbury Tales* can be found in the tales themselves. Chaucer writes in the dialect of late Middle English. While Gilpen writes in contemporary English, the tales include so much colloquial military English that the book ends with a glossary called "The Barstool Dictionary." According to the *Oxford English Dictionary,* one meaning for" tale" that enters Olde English circa 1200 is "A story or narrative, true or fictitious, drawn up so as to interest or amuse, or to preserve the history of a fact or incident; a literary composition cast in narrative form." Let me draw your attention to the phrase "to interest or amuse," for the most remembered of Chaucer's tales are those written in the genre of fabliaux, comic tales that include indelicate, irreverent, and bawdy humor. All of the tales in *Tales from the Green Side* involve such humor and the reader can't help but laugh out loud and then silently chide themselves for laughing, and then laugh some more. In a book of short stories about and dedicated to Sailors and Marines, you might wonder, why humor? Humor incites laughter. Comedian Milton Berle is credited with proclaiming that "laughter is the best medicine." Over a century before Berle, the Romantic poet George Gordon, Lord Byron recommended to "Always laugh when you can. It is cheap medicine". Humor is a powerful antidote to what ails us, whether sorrow or trauma, trials and tribulations, pain or loss. Humor allows us to present to others our vulnerable, human selves and to commiserate with as we laugh with the vulnerable, human selves of others. Humor, when well-intentioned and well-done, both presents and preserves our individual and collective humanity as we laugh and, sometimes cry, together.

Humor also offers a bridge between Gilpen's tales of the exploits and foibles of the Sailors and Marines whose stories appear in this volume. And while Gilpen's intended audience is members of the military community, writing as a humorist offers us civilian readers a bridge to cross so that we can get a glimpse of the "green side". I hope that you will consider these words my invitation for you to cross that bridge and experience *Tales from the Green Side*.

Catherine R. Mintler Ph.D.

Senior Lecture in the Edith Kinney Gaylord Expository Writing Program

Affiliate faculty in Women's and Gender Studies and the Carceral Studies Consortium at the University of Oklahoma

Co-founder, Oklahoma Prison Writers and Artists Foundation (OPWAF)

Norman, Oklahoma

Dispatch from Key West, Florida

July 23, 2000 – and – something…
Key West, Florida

Hey Senior,

Hoping this letter finds you well! First, Rob and I want to apologize for falling off the face of the earth. As you know, when we left Jacksonville, we headed south, following US 17 until we reached US 1. Along the way, we made a stop by Bobby's Blues Bar and Lounge. We got the chance to meet Master Guns Norton. He was cool as hell. We appreciate the introduction. We spent a couple of weeks hanging out with all the paramedics, EMTs, firemen, nurses, and other first responders who trickled in and out. Their stories, just like your guys, are funny as hell. Like Twain said… *Truth is stranger than fiction*. We walked away with so many stories we will be able to write a whole series of damn books.

Speaking of books, in this package, we've sent you the first copy of our first book, *Tales from the Green Side - Volume #1*. It has a half dozen stories we heard the first two nights we were in J-ville, i.e., Stanley's hope of being the next big action movie star, him describing what a corpsman is, the Preacher and the Padre, etc. I hope you enjoy them. It is the first of a series of books we have coming. The series is called the *Barstool Short-Story Anthology Series*. We have enough stories to write a couple more volumes of *Tales from the Green Side*. Before we do, we have been working on *Tales from the Back of the Bus* about the shit that happens in EMS and *Tales from the ER* we want to finish.

In the meantime, the two of us bought a couple of live-aboard sailboats. We are currently anchored off Stock Island. We've made the Florida Keys our AO for now. So, if you get down this way, make sure you call us! Hell, mini-lobster season is in a couple of weeks. It would be great to see you. You should load up the pups, grab Little Joe, weigh anchor, sail that Jeanneau down here, and hang out! Maybe we can get a couple of bottles of Hemingway Dark and head for the Straights on a fishing boat with our sights set on marlin or sailfish. Who knows - maybe the ghosts of Papa and the Pilar will bless us. Until next time, be well and be safe, my friend. We hope you enjoy the reading.

Hope to talk soon,

John S. & Rob A.

P.S. I forgot, a couple of weeks ago, we were up at a fishing shack in Islamorada having a couple of drinks. We had been in the backcountry fly fishing and ran into a guy who knew you. He claimed he served with you, in his words, "before you got old, soft, and lost all your military bearing." His name was Walt Claborn. Said he worked for Homeland Security or something — a nice guy.

Oh, as you probably already know, the crew he runs with are some genuine characters - somewhere between 'steely-eyed missile men' and just escaped from the looney bin - not sure which... If I could write their story, I would have a #1 best seller.

Anyway, take care, my friend!

Prologue

Fate chooses your relations, you choose your friends...

Jacques Delille[1]

1500
Thursday
Jack's BAS Bar & Grill
Hwy 17
Jacksonville, NC

"Welcome to Jack's BAS Bar and Grill. Please take a seat anywhere you please, and I'll be with you in a minute," a welcoming voice from the gentleman behind the bar shouted out as we walked inside the door. I acknowledge him with a thank you as we walk towards the old oak bar. The place is cozy and dimly lit for this time of day. The walls were adorned with old pictures of men and women in uniform, antique WWII recruiting posters, a brass ship's bell in the middle behind the bar, and what I assume to be old military uniforms hung in various places throughout. A sign points the way to the *Head* and the two pool tables in the back. An old-school jukebox was spinning a vinyl 45 rpm. *Wow, I didn't know they*

---

[1] [1] "Following the Equator."
https://www.goodreads.com/quotes/4650-truth-is-stranger-than-fiction-but-it-is-because-fiction

still existed. I assumed they were all CDs now. The song that dropped took me back home, and I doubt the radio plays Al Berry much anymore…

> *Once, I knew a Sailor who kept his sails in the wind…*[2]
> *His eyes searched the horizon…*
> *For places, he's never been.*
>
> *He'd say, "Everybody's looking for something."*
> *We all want what is free,*
> *But you only get what you pay for,*
> *you always end up where you're meant to be.*
>
> *And there's freedom in not knowing*
> *What the water has in store*
> *Home is where I'm standing*
> *What man could ask for more?*
> *So keep one eye on the water and one eye on the shore.*
> *Jesus, keep a light on for me*
> *In case I'm blown off course.*
>
> *Every Sailor has a story,*

---

[2] The Sailor written by Al Berry

But the theme is always the same

When you ride the waves in uncharted waters,

You learn to love the game...

And sometimes the waves are gentle,

They'll caress you like a loving hand,

Sometimes they try to break you,

So you learn to make a stand.

And there's freedom in not knowing

What the water has in store

Home is where I'm standing

What man could ask for more?

So keep one eye on the water and one eye on the shore.

Jesus, keep a light on for me

In case I'm blown off course.

It seems like yesterday

When they told me he was gone.

I guess I thought he'd live forever.

Now who will carry on?

He told me once about a man that could walk on water

So drowning men would know

There's a place for those who pray.

Well. I hope that's where he goes...

For a minute there, it reminded me of growing up back in Oklahoma and my old man.

No one else was in the place except for two old dogs – a little white one, a mini-schnauzer maybe, lying on top of the bar in an old, round dog bed near the register. The other, a colossal ass lion of a dog. I have no idea what he is. Massive is an understatement. Some type of mastiff - I don't really know. He is tan with some black around his face and ears. It stands over knee high. Like I said, massive! You can obviously see he has a six-inch ridge back of hair that probably stands straight up if he is pissed. I know for sure, it has a big blockhead, and it could eat the other one, eat it in one bite. Of that, I have no doubt.

"Hi, I am Jack, owner, operator, sole proprietor, short-order fry cook, head bottle washer, bartender, janitor, and part-time behind-the-bar therapist, at your service. What can I get for you two?" Obviously, seeing us look at the massive lion dog, "Oh, don't mind ol' Cooper over there. He just looks tough, but he's a 180 pound teddy bear! Just don't let him lay on ya! Now Cookie down there," pointing toward the white dog laying on the bar, "aka the Monster, on the other hand, she is just a cranky old CURMUDGEON! You gotta watch her, at least till she gets to know ya!" As he finished speaking, he began to laugh while wiping down the bar in front of us.

"Pleasure to meet you," I said, "This is Rob, and I'm John." Taking turns, each shaking his hand. "What kinda' IPAs do you have on tap?" I asked, inquiring what type of beers he had on hand.

He let out a loud, jolly Santa Claus-like laugh that filled the empty space of the bar, then pointed towards the wall to the right of the mirror behind the bar. "Son, I take it you've never been to my place before."

Shaking my head, no, " No, sir, we haven't. Why?" trying to figure out what he is pointing to. It was a sign on the wall. It read in big, bold letters, *'Jack's BAS Rules'*.

"Well, Son, I keep it pretty simple around here, *Jack's Rules*, they keep things flowing, …KISS, son KISS," Jack said, as Cookie got up, made a huge arching stretch before walking down the bar top. She started to nudge my hand with her nose.

"KISS?" I asked, confused, running my hand down the pup's back.

"Keep it Simple, Son, Keep it Simple. She likes you. She wants you to pet her," he tells me as he scratches her head.

I began scratching Cookie behind the ears, "Rules?" I asked.

"Yep," Pointing towards the giant sign on the wall behind the bar, he started reading...

"**<u>RULE No. 1.</u>** Jack's Bar, Jack's Rules No Questions!

<u>RULE No. 2.</u> If there is any doubt, always refer to RULE #1!

RULE No. 3. Leave your Worries at the Door!

RULE No. 4. Jack *ONLY* serves Coors, Budweiser, Shiner, and Papst Blue Ribbon Beer (if you drink that yuppy, light in your loafer, foo-foo beer, keep driving).

RULE No. 5. Jack *ONLY* Serves Capt., Sailor Jerry, Bacardi, Jack, Jim, Jose, Wild Turkey, and on *occasion* Crown (subject to change on Jack's mood).

RULE No. 6. Three Drink Limit - Number FOUR, *drop* your keys with a $10 bill in the Jar - *Nobody Drinks and Drives on My Watch! Period end of Question!*

RULE No. 7. NO Fighting, YOU want to Fight, SEE ME, WE WILL GO OUTSIDE. *Enough Said!*

RULE No. 8. Knock the Cue Ball off the table – $5 in the Juke & $5 in the Toys-4-Tots kitty jar. *NO exceptions!*

RULE No. 9. JACK CAN CHANGE *THE* RULES AT ANY TIME!"

Looking at Rob, who shrugged his shoulders, I turned back towards Jack, "Two pints of Shiner it is!" I tell him, laughing to myself.

Jack replied, "Two Shiners, Coming up!" As he grabbed two pint glasses from behind the bar.

Rob put his card on the bar to pay for the drinks.

"First rounds on the house. Welcome to my place!" Jack said with a grin as wide as Texas as he dropped a coaster on the bar and sat the beer in front of us.

Conferring our gratitude, "Thanks, Jack, you did not have to do that! We appreciate it, though. We have not had this kind of welcome anywhere we have been yet." Then I put the glass to my lips and began to dust the top off. *The beer was cold. I'll give him that.*

Jack answered, "My pleasure, boys!" as he went back to wiping down the bar. Cookie returned to her spot at the end of the bar, curling up in her bed.

"What brings you boys to town?" Jack asked. "By the length of your hair, you're not on active duty. Thats long even for Navy grooming standard. Since I've never seen you before, guessin' you're not locals."

"We are just passing through," I said, "riding through the southeast on our bikes, and I blew out my rear tire this morning… ended up cutting up my drive belt too! Couldn't find a new one anywhere. The Harley dealer said he couldn't get a new one till next Tuesday. So here we are. Got a room at the Triangle Inn down the street. The desk clerk recommended the food here, so here we are," shrugging my shoulders. "What's good? We are starving!" I asked, looking around for a menu. "You have a menu we can look at?"

"Onion cheddar burgers with fried jalapenos on Hawaiian bread buns, fresh-cut fries, smothered in freshly grated block cheddar cheese... it's my personal favorite." He put the Monster on the floor, came around the bar, and began taking down the chairs from the tables and putting them on the floor.

Rob, looking at me, raised two fingers in the air, "Two of those sound perfect!"

"Two #2's coming up," as he makes his way back towards the kitchen, followed by the Cooper and the Monster.

I stood up and started walking around, looking at the pictures on the walls, Marines and Sailors, mainly. Some from Vietnam, the Middle East. Some from WWI - I recognize the Doughboys. WWII Marines in the South Pacific, and Korea, based on the uniform and the snow and ice. Some had names. Some had dates. Some were labeled KIA, a few were MIA. "Rob, look at all this stuff. I've never seen anything like it!"

He looked over at me, "I know it. This place is a military history museum."

"I wonder what the story is with this place," I said as we walked around the bar, in awe of the pictures and memorabilia on the walls.

Ten, maybe fifteen minutes passed before Jack reappeared with two plates covered with home-cut fries and two of the biggest damn burgers I have ever seen. Cooper and the Monster were close on his heels. He sat the burgers on the bar top, and we returned to our bar stools.

"Ketchup, mustard, Heinz 57, salt, and pepper you'll find at the end of the bar." He placed a silverware roll in front of the plate. "Here are some utensils," he said as he wiped his hands on the towel he kept on his shoulder.

I wrapped both my hands around the burger to start eating. After taking a couple of bites I exclaimed, "Damn, Jack, the clerk was not joking when she said you had the best burger and coldest brews in town!"

"You boys want another Shiner?" Jack asked, simultaneously grabbing the empty glasses and headed to the tap, both of us nodding yes.

Returning with our freshly filled glasses, "Glad you like it, boys, I'll let you get to eating. Let me know if you need anything, ya hear?" he says with a massive grin on his face.

With a mouth half full of food, "Jack, what's the deal with this place? It's not like any bar we've ever been in before?" I asked.

"Really not much to it. I served 24 years in the Navy and retired as a Senior Chief. My wife died two years before I got out from breast cancer. That's her in the picture there on the mirror," pointing to a faded photo of a much younger version of Jack in a blue Navy uniform and a woman in a white dress. He looked like the cartoon character on a box of Crackerjacks.

"I'm very sorry to hear that," I said empathetically.

"Don't be. Kids were grown and had families of their own. Didn't really need me, so I opened this place. To an outsider, it's just another bar, but for the Sailors and Marines who walk through those doors, especially my regulars, it's a refuge, a safe harbor from the day-to-day grind of military life, hence the name BAS." Jack continues talking as he puts the last two chairs under the tables and turns back towards the bar.

"BAS? I never heard of a BAS." Turning and looking at Rob, who is shaking his head, "No."

"What does it mean?" I asked Jack.

"Battalion Aid Station, it's what Corpsmen and Marines call their medical casualty collection and treatment area. The area where they treat their wounded in the field when deployed," he answered.

Still not sure what he was talking about, we both nod our heads in agreement. "Jack, what did you do in the Navy?" I asked.

"I was an FMF Hospital Corpsman most of my career, and from the look on your faces, neither of you have any idea what that is. Simple explanation, I was a combat medic with Marine infantry units." Leaning against the bar, looking at us. Senior asked, "What about you guys? How do you pay the bills?"

"Me, I am a freelance illustrator and cartoonist," Rob said as he pushed his empty plate away from himself. "By the way, that", pointing at the plate, "was amazing Jack!"

Rob turned to look at me. "I am mostly a content writer, i.e., I get paid to help others write about anything they can't put *pen to paper* themselves. But I want to be more than that! I have been wanting to write my first book. So, we decided to take this trip. We wanted to get out of our *bubble*. See America from the back of our Harleys. We are hoping to find inspiration. Something unique others have not written about. Something different Rob can capture in his drawings and I can bring to life in words. I like to think of myself as a humorist, which is not always the easiest thing to express, much less get published." I had to stop myself. I was rambling. I hate it when I do that. Rob was sitting there laughing at me, as usual.

"A humorist?" Jack asked as he grabbed our plates and stacked them together.

"Yeah, you know, like Mark Twain, Will Rogers, Garrison Keillor and Lake Wobegon. I am not a comedian. I want to write stories that make people laugh but also remind them of something that was good and meaningful in their lives. I know it sounds idealistic and naïve," I said, shaking my head and shrugging my shoulders. A little disappointed, doubting myself.

Throwing the towel over his shoulder, he said, "Son, do you believe in fate?" Jack asked, looking at me with a serious and intense face.

I answered, "Yeah. Maybe. Why?" shrugging my shoulders, looking at Jack, a little puzzled and curious about why he was asking.

His grin cracked, and he opened up his thoughts, "Boys, your flat tire was fate! It's Thursday. Your bike won't be ready till

Tuesday morning at the earliest, so you're in J-ville for the next five nights. Right?" Looking at us, we both nodded yes. "It was not by chance you walked into Jack's ol' place! That I can guarantee. There is no such thing as coincidences! If you boys come back in a couple of hours and every night till you leave. Buy the men and women who call this place theirs a few rounds, I'll introduce you to the *right* ones. If by the time you're ready to ride out of town Tuesday," looking pretty damn sure of himself, "you two do not have enough material to fill at least two books, not only is your tab on the house, I'll cover the bill at Triangle Inn too!" He stuck out his hand and said, "Deal?" A few seconds of silence passed, "Now, just remember what your Mark Twain said"...

"What's that," I asked.

"Truth is stranger than fiction, but it is because fiction is obliged to stick to possibilities. Truth isn't!" hand still out.

I looked at Rob, who was nodding his head, smiling, and I turned as I laughed.

"DEAL!"

ABCs, Sucking Chest Wounds, and Emergency Cric's...

Truth is so hard to tell, it sometimes needs fiction to make it plausible.

Francis Bacon[3]

1830
Thursday
Jack's BAS Bar & Grill
Hwy 17
Jacksonville, NC

By 1830, when I pulled into Jack's BAS Bar and Grill, there were only a couple of POVs in the lot. Senior's souped-up Dodge 3500, two that belonged to a couple of *boots* - you know those Marines and Sailors fresh to the fleet, and a little sedan I had never seen before. That's not a bad thing. I could use a little peace and quiet. No *admin squirrels* barking orders in my ear. I thought I was never going to get out of the damn office today. I hate admin duty! I didn't volunteer for the *green side* just to shuffle papers into stupid medical records all damn day! Screw it! It doesn't matter. Not right now. Not tonight anyway. I damn sure

---

[3] The Most Famous Movie Line and Quotes in Action Films. Access on 01/23/2023 at https://movieweb.com/the-most-famous-movie-lines-and-quotes-in-action-films/#quot-you-39-ve-got-to-ask-yourself-one-question-do-i-feel-lucky-well-do-ya-punk-quot

don't want to get my balls busted by Senior for breaking one of his sacred rules, especially Rule No. 3... Leave your damn troubles, worries, problems, woes, etc., etc., etc., blah blah blah. My opinion - leave your BULLSHIT at the door, and that's precisely what I am going to do tonight!

I opened the door and was immediately greeted by Cooper, standing guard duty again! To the uninitiated, Cooper is a 180 pound plus Anatolian Shepherd who has struck fear into many a man and/or woman's soul. Just his size alone is menacing. Truthfully, unless you're hurting someone's kid, a woman, or one of his two sidekicks – Harley "Bob Marley" or the Monster. Cooper just wants table scraps, and his head scratched. I would hate to see Senior's dog food bill. He probably goes through 25 lbs. of dog food every 6-7 days, has to! I scratched his head and looked around the bar. From the back, running as fast as he could, tongue hanging out, comes Harley "Bob Marley" – the friendliest salt and pepper mini-Schnauzer you've ever seen! He loves everyone. The way he runs around the bar loving on people, I think he's gotten into Little Joe's brownies a time or two. If you know what I mean.

Little Joe is the part-time cook and janitor who works for Senior. Everyone thinks he's from Jamaica with his grey dreads, his keen affinity for reggae music, and his left-handed cigarettes. However, he insists he's from St. John. Who knows for sure? It doesn't matter to me as long as he keeps cooking his jerked chicken every Tuesday and Saturday night. He and Senior bonded over to their love of Jerry Garcia, The Dead, and barbecuing competitions... *a friend of the devil is a friend of mine*. I looked around the corner toward the back, I didn't know the two boots playing pool or the two guys in the booth by the jukebox.

I turned my attention toward the man backing the bar, "Hey Senior!" The Monster in her bed near the register raised her head, scanned her domain like a mountain lion on a perch searching the terrain for prey. Stretched a huge stretch, and laid back down. My presence was an intrusion. An interruption of her *nap time*, nothing more.

Shutting the cooler door, then turning around, grinning, his smile. The one that never fails to illuminate the room. "Hey Tobey, How the hell are you, son?" as he dried his huge hands off with the towel he had over his shoulder and stuck out his hand. Seniors' customary salutation of friendship.

I took his hand with a firm shake, "Better now that I am here, Senior! That's for *damn sure!*" You can always count on Senior being here with a smile, a firm handshake, and a cold beer. He's guaranteed to have the Dead on vinyl spinning several times an hour. It's an unwritten rule anyone who frequents this establishment knows! Cooper followed me to the bar and nudged my leg. I reached down to pet him. Cooper and Senior are genuinely meant for each other – both gentle giants. Senior's pushing 6'4", tipping the scales at 250 to 260 lbs. - not an ounce of fat on him. He is in his 50's. Never heard anyone really say. Still, he gets up every morning, rain or shine, at 0545, laces up his shoes, and runs at least 3 miles. More if he is "feeling it." Once he has done his *road time*, he hits the gym for an hour of weights. I promise you, that old-timer can pull more weight than most Marines stationed at Lejeune. He is a damn beast who can be intimidating with his ponytail and handlebar 'stache. The kind even Sam Elliot would be envious of. I am not going to fuck with him, and I feel sorry for the dumbass who does! I've only heard stories from guys who served under him. They said he was a hard ass. A motivated hard charger who drank the green side Kool-Aid straight from the tap! The scuttlebutt is he was a straight shooter, always fair and impartial, and always there for his guys. An NCO who was unafraid to lay it all on the line for his sailors. I guess that's why we call him Senior and not Master Chief.

"A Yellow Jacket and a Captain's Mast! Please, kind sir!" I requested as I took a seat at the bar.

"One of those days, was it?" Senior asked as he grabbed a glass and a bottle of Captain Morgan's Spiced Rum from the shelf behind the bar.

"One of those weeks, Senior! Been stuck on admin duty all week! It's been months, and Sox is still pissed at me!" I replied, shrugging my shoulders as I grabbed a handful of the bar nuts out of a bowl on top of the bar. Senior just smiled, then laughed and shook his head.

"Excuse me, sir, I don't mean to interrupt, but what is a Captain Mast? I don't think I have ever heard of that specific drink," asked the stranger sitting at the booth.

I turned around to see who had asked the question, "John, Rob, I want to introduce you to one of the guys we were talking about earlier today. Guys, this is HM3 Tobias Thomas Stanley, FMF Hospital Corpsman extraordinaire. We just call him Tobey," Senior said with a sense of joy I seldom hear in his voice when he introduces people. *Wonder what that shit is all about?*

I turned around and looked at Senior, who winked, nodded, and said, "I've got to finish stocking the cooler. I'll get you your Colorado Kool-Aid in a minute." I grabbed the drink in my left hand, stood up, and walked over to their booth, sticking out my right hand, "Pleasure to meet the both of you. Any friend of the Senior is a friend of mine."

John asked, "Would you like to pull up a chair and join us?" as he held out his hand in a gesture conferring me to join them. Harley had found his way to the booth and was sitting next to Rob, enjoying having his head rubbed, tongue hanging out, panting - a smiling dog for sure.

Senior coming around the bar with my Yellow Jacket in hand, "Tobey, Rob here is an illustrator, and John is a humorist. They're here looking for sea stories to write about for their new book. I told them there are enough sea stories floating around this old place to fill a whole damn series of books!"

"That's a no shitter right there, Senior!" Turning towards the two new friends Senior had just introduced me to, "So I'll answer your first question, then you're going to have to elaborate on this mission you are on." I took a drink from my Yellow Jacket, looked at my two new friends, and they nodded "yes" in agreement.

"Well, in the blue water Navy, a Captain's Mast occurs when you've screwed the pooch, and you're standing in front of the old man," I said, using my hands to help convey my point.

"Old man?" Rob asked.

"Yeah, the commanding officer, in the Navy, it refers to the captain of the ship. In the Corps, it is the CO, the unit's commanding officer, and he is handing out his brand of non-judicial punishment. It can be as simple as picking up butts in the quad or doing old school Navy corrosion control - i.e., painting the damn ship haze grey and underway, whether it needs it or not! And the Corps favorite, CCU... the good ole Corrective Custodial Unit. Making big rocks into little rocks to readjust your attitude..." Turning and walking away, smiling and shaking his head, Senior knew those two had already swallowed the hook and didn't even know it yet.

"So, back to the drink. It's spiced rum. Usually Captain Morgan's, and pineapple juice. It goes down fast and smooth. Before long, you're... well. Tomorrow you're standing in front of the old man answering for things you do not remember doing.

Still, there are enough assholes, excuse me. The appropriate legal terminology would be - witnesses. Well, there is no need to argue!" I said while shrugging my shoulders before I wet my whistle.

Looking a little puzzled, "Then why drink it?" John asked.

"Why? Because you will not have a hangover the next day, that's why? As Lance Corporal Frankie the Freak says - *Operators Gotta Operate!*' I said, then I began laughing, an inside joke.

"A round of Captain Masts, please, Jack," John said as he made a circle with his arm.

"It's your turn boys," trying not to sound patronizing, "tell me about this mission from God you two are on?" I asked, wondering if these two caught my Jake and Elwood reference.

John looks straight at me with no expression, just this blank stare…. "Tobey, it's like this… it's a hundred and six miles to Chicago, we got a full tank of gas, half a pack of cigarettes, it's dark… and we're wearing sunglasses." Then he turns to Rob.

Rob looks at him just as expressionless, "Hit it!" Then they both crack the fuck up!

Damn, I love these two! Smart asses! These guys just might be ok! "Hey, Senior, we got us a pair of wise guys here."

"Seriously, we just want to write American stories. Stories about the heart and soul of the people that are the fabric of who we are as a country. Stories Rob can draw cartoons about. Stories I can write about that are open, honest, raw – about human nature. I want to write about things the average American wouldn't see on TV or read about in *Time* or *People* magazines. The catch is it has to have humor in it. We believe there is enough travesty, pain, and loss. We want to provide some comic relief from our work," as

Rob shakes his head in agreement. "Not to be rude, but we are not looking for gory war stories. I hope that doesn't offend you?"

"Not at all, brother, not at all! I understand completely! You're not looking for *war stories*. You're looking for what those of us privileged souls who have the honor of carrying on the burden of the altruistic and noble traditions of naval service refer to as *sea stories*!"

With a tilted head, "Sea stories?" John asked.

"Sea stories!" Shaking my head, yes. "You know the difference between a fairy tale and a sea story?" I asked to make sure they knew they didn't offend me.

They both shook their heads no. "Well, boys, a fairy tale starts with…Once upon a time, and a sea story, it starts with…There I was!" Then as we all three started laughing. "Last week, Corporal Glass and I were joking we should write a book about all the crazy shit we do. You know the crazy shenanigans that happens. But I said no one would believe us!"

John gave me a look that's kinda' creepy. Maybe that's the look of a creative genius, but what do I know? Suddenly he exclaimed, "That's exactly what we are looking for!!" while raising both hands into the air like a member of the East Marietta Baptist Church congregation singing gospel on Sunday morning with Brother Ray rocking the pulpit, the Good Book in hand.

Rob grabbed a small bag containing a bunch of pencils and a drawing pad. "We're ready when you are."

"Ready for what?" I asked.

"Tell us a sea story," Rob said, putting on a pair of glasses from a case he had in his bag.

"Okay…" I said, "You want me to tell you sea stories?" I asked surprised.

"Yeah, why not?" Rob asked.

"Tobey, why don't you start by telling them what a Green Side Corpsman is," Senior yelled from behind the bar.

"That's a great place to start. You guys are combat medics, right?" John asked as he pushed play on his tape recorder.

"First, let's get something straight. We are Hospital Corpsmen, not Combat Medics," I said with inflection in my voice to make a distinction between the two. "Got it?"

Looking a little startled, they both replied, "Got it!"

"Combat Medics are those medical maggots who take care of legs and other nastiness in the Army and Air Force," I said, adjusting my shoulders. "Corpsmen, specifically, FMF 8404 Corpsmen are a rare breed of human. We are those *divine Men and Women* chosen by the Hand of God himself. Created on the 8th Day after He had rested to make sure his *earthly bound warriors, Marines,* have *Guardian Angels* to accompany them into hell. To wage war on the demons and evil of this world and the next. We are *Devil Docs* forged from the iron of Gabriel, the Archangel's sword. We have chosen to live a savage and spartan life. We become intimate with violence, killing, pain, and suffering. Our acquaintances are the cold, the dirt, loneliness, and filth. Our bond with our Marines is deeper. The losses greater! The one thing we know and we embrace is the *SUCK*. Gentleman, Devil Docs don't nearly survive. We *thrive in chaos*!"

"Damn, dat deep man! Deep!" I heard from the kitchen door, as I looked and saw Little Joe sharpening his knife with a long sharpening steel. He looked at Senior, smiled, shook his head, and returned to the kitchen.

Rob was busy doodling. John was taking notes when he looked up and said. "Wow... Ok! I agree with what Little Joe." Then he asked, "What kind of training do you go through that's different from the *other guys?*"

"Other guys? You mean those Medical Maggots, sorry, Army Medics?" Clearing my throat, "Let me make an injection here. I am not talking about 18 Deltas. Those are some hard mother fuckers, no question. They have my mad respect, period!" stopping to clarify.

"What are 18 Deltas?" Rob asked as he took a break from his frantic doodling and looked up at me.

"18 Delta is the designation for the Special Forces Medical Sergeant. Those gents are no joke. They are the real deal, brothers. I promise you the Grim Reaper has nightmares about them when he sleeps!" I said being as serious as I could, not because I was being sarcastic, but because I believed every word of it! I have been through the goat lab, and I have seen them in action.

"With the exception of the 18 Delta's, the Army does not send their medics through additional combat-specific training as the Navy and Marine Corps does. The 8404 designator is a C

school, advanced training beyond combat medicine/EMT." Back to talking with my hands as usual. "In Corps school - it's like EMT school for civilians. You focus on your ABCs." I could tell by the looks on their faces they were lost. "You know, airway, breathing, and circulation. The first thing you do is open the airway and make sure you have a patent airway. Surely you boys have taken a CPR class, right?" Looking at them, nodding yes, made me think maybe they had.

"Then make sure they have a pulse, etc., etc., etc. You get the picture, right?" I asked, attempting to prod an answer with my hands,

"Basic first aid?" John asked.

"Exactly, basic first aid! Throw in a rectal check or two, an STD workup, how to give Rocephin shots and vaccinations, and 14 weeks later, you're a newly minted Quad Zero (0000) Corpsman," throwing both hands up in the air, "or in the Chair Force a medic, and if you're in the Army - you're a *Combat Medic.*"

Leaning back, I finish off my Yellow Jacket and turn towards the bar, "Senior, can I get a #2? Please?" Turning back to Rob and John, "You two had dinner?"

"Jack, we'll take two as well. Please," John asked, raising two fingers in the air above his head so Senior could see.

"Three #2's on their way out!" Senior yelled, as he headed towards the back. Harley jumped down and made a beeline towards the kitchen as well. Maybe that's where Little Joe keeps the brownies, smiling to myself.

The jukebox had quit playing, "Boys, the box has run dry, give me a sec," as I stood up and walked over and stared at the playlist. Being a juke that only plays 45s, you're limited to songs before 1990 and the owner's tastes, i.e., Senior Chief Jackson "Jack" Samuel Taylor, Deadhead, with an island flair of Bob

Marley and Jimmy Buffett. Senior lives on a Jeanneau Sun Odyssey 44 DS, a 44-foot sailboat he has docked at a friend's somewhere past the Sneads Ferry bridge. He keeps a nice center console docked out behind the bar and runs back and forth every night. "Let's keep the cook happy and rack up some Dead, Buffett, Skynyrd, Allman Brothers, and top it off with some Marshall Tucker. Sound good to you?" I asked as I dropped a $10 roll of quarters in the slot and began to push *1A: A Pirate Looks at 40 - Jimmy Buffett*, seemed fitting.

Sitting back in my chair, "Where were we?" I said before picking up my Captain's Mast and finishing it off as well.

"What makes 8404s different from the other medical maggots?" John asked as he checked the notes on his big yellow notepad.

John and his notepad reminded me of the Big Chief Tablets I had when I was a kid in grade school. "Oh yeah, the difference. The difference is FMSS - Field Medical Service School. There are two, one out in San Diego for those Hollywood candy asses and here at Camp Johnson, just down the road." Pointing towards the northeast, I said, "Just make a right at the Beirut Memorial. Have you guys been to the Beirut Memorial yet?"

"Yeah, we went earlier today. The lone Marine standing watch is eerie. Like he is on guard, protecting the ghosts of his brothers," Rob said as he put down his pencil and looked up at me.

I think he understood the meaning and sacredness of the memorial. I like these guys more and more.

"Good, a lot of those pictures to the left of the jukebox there are of many of the men on that memorial wall," I said, pointing out the picture frames on the wall.

"Really, where did they come from? How did Jack come by them all?" John asked.

"He took them. Senior was a corpsman assigned to the 24th Marine Amphibious Unit," I said. Judging by the looks on John's and Rob's faces, Senior's credibility was now firmly established.

"Jack was in Lebanon when the Marine barracks were bombed in 1983?" Rob asked as he looked at me and then back at the pictures on the wall.

"Yeah, but he wasn't at the barracks. He was on the USS Iwo Jima, LPH-2, a support ship off the Lebanese coast. He was there for the aftermath and the recovery of the Marines and Sailors from 1/8," I said, shaking my head. It was a somber moment, always is, but back to the mission at hand.

"Anyways, FMSS, it's where the newly assigned blue side and boot Corpsmen learn to be Marines in eight weeks. It's a rude awakening for most. Navy boot camp, for the most part, is bullshit compared to the Marines P.I. in South Carolina or Hollywood's Mount Motherfucker in San Diego," stopping to take a drink of the fresh round Senior had just brought.

"P.I.? What's Hollywood got to do with Marines? Are they making some kind of movie?" John asked as he scrolled the page of his notebook.

I snorted in my beer. Man, these two really have no clue about the culture or the life. "P.I. is short for Parris Island, where Marine Boot Camp is for all those east of the Mississippi. And well, *all* those who graduate boot camp at the P.I. refer to the Marine Boot Camp in San Diego, California, as *Hollywood* and those who graduate from there as *Hollywood Marines*.

"Oh..., Ok. Got it", John said, shaking his head.

"It is a rude awakening because you're living in stupid-ass WWII, open-squad bay barracks, in bunk beds, and you have two primary instructors per platoon. One psycho-ass Marine Sergeant or Staff Sergeant who has grandeur notions of being Gunnery Sergeant Hartman. You know, the badass Drill Instructor from *Full Metal Jacket.* The other instructor, a 2nd Class or 1st Class Corpsman who has, at best, like Senior over there - someone who drank the *Green Side* Kool-Aid. At worst, is pissed off at the world because their career counselor fucked them. Either way, their job is to make your life as miserable as they fucking can." Deploying my best knife hand to impress upon my new friends the ability of these two demonic, sadistic individuals to turn your entire world upside down for eight long, miserable weeks.

"During these eight weeks, you learn how to properly maintain and shoot to kill with your M-16 out to 500 yards using

CAREER COUNSELOR

iron sights and your Beretta M-9 semi-automatic handgun. By the time you graduate FMSS, Corpsmen are more than just *Heartbreakers* and *Life Savers*. Gents, we are *steely-eyed killers* if you come between a wounded Marine and us!" I said, grabbing my drink, nodding my head as I winked at Rob and smiled! I could tell these two were thinking – WTF did I get myself into?

"What about the medicine part? It has to be more than just basic first aid and STD checks?" Rob asked without looking up from whatever he was doodling.

Rob has not really stopped even to take a drink of his beer or Captain's Mast. I guess we'll soon see how good this cat truly is. "FMSS is where we get into combat medicine's nuts and bolts. We focus on treating a pneumothorax. You know, that's when you pop a hole in your lung, and the inside of your chest fills up with air. Let me tell you. It's brutal! You can't breathe because every time you breathe in air, it just goes inside of you, and the pressure, well, it's the pressure starts to squeeze your lungs." I picked up the empty beer can and crushed it in my left hand for effect.

"Rob, if you're not going to drink that beer, I'll drink it so it doesn't get hot. I'll get you another one, a cold one. Nothing worse than a hot beer. Well, that's not true. No beer is worse than a hot beer." I imparted my little bit of two-cent wisdom. Rob shook his head no in acknowledgment. and I reach across the table and grab his lukewarm beer.

Picking up where I left off, "John, on your Big Chief Tablet," John looks at me like, WTF are you talking about, "On your yellow Big Chief Tablet", pointing to his notepad, "Make a column for things to circle back to, OK?" In acknowledgment, John nods, and I say "Write Carlsberg, Probably the World's Greatest Beer. Got it?"

"Got it. What's this column for exactly?" John asked with a furrowed brow wondering what the hell I was thinking. I know that look. I get it a lot! Especially from HM2 Sox.

"Sea stories, brother, sea stories! Things to talk about, but I am trying not to lose focus on this sea story by going down a rabbit hole, if you know what I mean," as I stand up and walk up to the bar. "Senior, can I get another round, and any ETA, on those burgers?"

"Little Joe is in the back, peeling some fresh potatoes he picked up at the farmers market today. Another 15 mikes or so. I see you're keeping our new friends entertained over there," Senior said as he put six Yellow Jackets on the bar top. "I know, put em' on your tab," laughing as he turned and walked back towards the kitchen.

"Back to important shit!" I shouted, turning my chair around backward so I could focus on my new friends and their mission from *GOD*. Over my shoulder, I heard Senior say, "Cooks," scratching her head, "the shit's gettin' serious now!" followed by his Santa Claus laugh. I turned and looked at him over my right shoulder with a raised brow and then a smile. I could see he was shaking his head as he was back to his bartending duties… Others were starting to drift in. I turned back to the business at hand. Rob was sharpening his bag of pencils. *That boy is obsessed, to say the least, and to my surprise, talented! His 8404 cartoon is freaking AMAZING.*

"So, when your lungs are getting the shit squeezed out of them like the can right there, you get what you call tracheal deviation When you roll up on that, the inner voice that drives your actions better be kicking your ass into high gear. Why do you ask? Because time is of the essence, boys! What I mean by tracheal deviation is," grabbing hold of my throat and wiggling it back and forth, "the pressure is building up so much all of your lungs are being shifted to one side and causing your trachea to shift the opposite way! We call that a *late sign*, and if you don't do something *sooner than later*, you're going to be *too damn late*! If you know what I mean."

Sitting on the edge of what I was saying, "What can you do to fix it?" John asked.

"That's easy! You just dart his chest!" I motioned with my right hand like I was throwing a dart as I reached down to grab my beer and take a drink!

"Dart his chest? You don't really stick darts in the chest? That sounds pretty damn painful and barbaric!" Rob asked as he looked at me over the top of his glasses, wondering if I was being serious or just full of shit.

"Not darts like you throw at a dart board," pointing to the dartboard in the back. "Darting is the slang for the medical procedure used to fix the problem - needle decompression. You take a 14-gauge IV catheter," using my right hand to point to the spot on my upper left chest. "You insert it just above the rib right here between the 2-3 rib mid-clavicular on the affected side. Do it right and the air comes rushing out like after removing a nail in

your tire on a hot summer day, and you can breathe again. It's really pretty damn simple if you stop and think about it."

"KISS!" John exclaimed.

Turning towards him, "Exactly! You're starting to catch on!" I told him to reinforce his moment of clarity. Trying to picture the process in his head, "How do you know which side to dart?" Rob asked.

"That's easy. Dart the chest wall on the opposite side of the trachea deviation." I tell them using my hands to demonstrate by moving my trachea back and forth.

"That's pretty freaking cool, Tobey! Do you do that often?" John asked.

"Not a lot, really. Seen it more often when I've been on the bus," I said as I tried to readjust my chair.

"Bus?" Rob asked confused trying to understand how public transportation just came into the conversation.

"Sorry. A bus is slang for an ambulance. I work civilian EMS some, volunteering for Richlands Rescue on my off time. It usually only happens when you have blunt force trauma to the chest, like a steering wheel, a bat, or crowbar, or from blast injuries, i.e., the overpressure from an explosion and your dumb ass gets blown into the wall or truck like you see on TV or some stupid shit like that!" I said, leaning back in the chair to take another drink.

Looking over my shoulder, I saw who was walking in the door, "Boys, this here is my running buddy. My ride or die! A brother from a different mother. Philly's own Lance Corporal, Frankie the Freak!" acknowledging my buddy Frankie Talibasco, who joined us at the booth!

"Wha's' yous up to, Doc?" Frankie asked as he reached down to pick up Harley, who had come running up to him.

"Brews and sea stories with a couple of Senior's buddies! Grab yourself a beer and join us if you want," I said, pulling a chair around.

"Sweet! I am waiting for Staff Sergeant Hart and his wife. She wants to introduce me to a friend. A girl she works with," Frankie said, smiling, pointing to himself with both his thumbs like the Fonz and trying not to drop Harley.

"She wants to introduce Lance Corporal Frankie the Freak to her friend? She must not be a very good friend!" I said and then started to laugh.

"Fuck you, Doc! Better me than some squid like you!" and flying me the double barrel bird. "I'll be back in a few. Get you boys anything?" Frankie asked. Everyone shook their heads no. Frankie turned and walked to the bar, followed by Harley.

"You guys are *friends?*" John asked.

"I'd take a bullet for him, and I know he would take one for me!" tapping my chest.

"Sounds more like he might put a bullet *in you!* You two have a strange way of expressing your friendship," Rob said as he pushes his glasses up on his face.

"The military breeds a type of bond most civilians will never understand. There are not enough words or books to explain it to them! Let me finish telling you about FMSS before Senior brings out those burgers." I leaned up on the back of the chair again.

"There are a couple of other things that are pretty important skills. The first is knowing how to fix a sucking chest wound! So, when a guy gets shot, stabbed, or catches a piece or two of shrapnel in the chest," again pointing to my chest. "Now, that hole has created a whole different set of problems than we had before. Now, we can't keep the air in the chest! So basically, you're suffocating cause you can't breathe. But again, if you have any critical thinking skills at all, it's an easy fix! Hell, we teach Marines to fix it; if they can fix it, any moron can do it! All you have to do is slap some form of plastic, i.e., ID card, or AED pad, and believe it or not, a damn sticky rat trap will work! You know, one of those great big mothers!" Holding my hands up, making about 6-inch x 6-inch square.

"The biggest mistake people make is not looking for the exit wound! You have gotta remember what goes in," and using my index finger, I point from the middle of my stomach with my right hand out to the left side, "usually comes out on the opposite side somewhere - creating an exit wound! And it's more likely than not, bigger than the hole on the side it went in on!" Using my left hand, I mimic an explosion on my left side to demonstrate an exit wound. "If you don't plug both, your Marine is DRT!"

"DRT?" John asks as he stops taking notes.

"DRT, Dead Right There!" Frankie butts in as he takes the seat behind me, setting down another round of Yellow Jackets for the group.

"Exactly! Thanks, brother!" Frankie lifts his beer and nods. The two new recruits do the same. "Once that is done, you can start to breathe again. The problem is now, we have a pneumothorax basically. So, you gotta watch for those same signs and symptoms and be prepared to fix the problem."

Using his hand to imitate throwing a dart, "Then you just dart them, right?" John asks.

"No, you've already got a hole, remember? You just have to lift the edge of whatever you placed on the entrance wound. The air will rush out. Wait until they breathe in and stick it back down. Pretty simple, except if you used that damn rat trap, now you've got a helluva a mess, and it might be easier just to dart them again. That's one of those tactical decisions you make when the issue arises." I laughed as I made a questioning motion with my hands.

"The other skill you need to be proficient in is the surgical cricothyrotomy technique! This is where using a scalpel with the precision of a trauma surgeon to make a very small opening in the neck here," pointing to the Adam's apple of my neck, "so that you can place an ET tube to secure an airway in extreme emergencies."

Excited, "Like on TV where they use a straw or ballpoint pen?" John asked.

"Sorta, but a straw and pen are not big enough to get the job done," I replied to John.

"Still, don't know why you guys insist on using those little wimpy-ass scalpels my kids play with at recess, Doc! Just man up and use your K-Bar! You'll never wonder if the holes are big enough!" exclaims Frankie, inserting his unsolicited two cents.

"Why? Because I don't want to contaminate my pristine blade with anything you morons might have in your blood like the clap or tetanus and such! That's why!" Never even looking to see his expression. I knew what it looked like. That happens when you

have broken as much bread as we have. Both John and Rob were looking at me, and I winked at them. They both shook their heads. I wonder what they're thinking. No, I am not. I know they're questioning their choices of dinner company; I am sure!

"That sounds like some amazing training…" John started to say.

"Hey boys, I hate to interrupt this meeting of the minds, but I have three #2's medium here," Senior yelled over the crowd as he and Little Joe came walking from the kitchen with three plates and a huge platter of fresh-cut fries. "Why don't you guys take a break from all this serious interrogation and enjoy it!"

"It's about damn time! I am starving. You know I have to have high-octane racing fuel," rubbing my belly, "on regular intervals to maintain this finely oiled love machine, Senior!" Laughing as Senior rolled his eyes at me. He began shaking his head, as usual. Smiling as he walked back towards the bar.

I turned towards John, "John, you know the trash talking earlier on the medics was just interservice rivalry bullshit, right?"

"You mean the medical maggots, Tobey?" laughing, "Yeah, I figured as much," as he put away his Big Chief Tablet and tape recorder.

"But you know why they call us Corpsmen and not medics, right?" John shook his head no. "Because medics need heroes, too!" He turned and looked at me. I winked, *"Let's Eat!"* Both John and Rob grinned. I stood up and turned my chair back around toward the table. I happened to glance at the drawings Rob had penciled out over the last 30 minutes. *Impressive!* I wonder if John can write half as well. I guess we'll see......

The Movie Star: Why Doc Only Gets to Go to the Pistol Range

"You've got to ask yourself one question:
Do I feel lucky? Well, do ya, punk?"

Inspector Harry Callahan[4]

2010
Thursday Night
Jack's BAS Bar & Grill
Hwy 17
Jacksonville, NC

Chris Ledoux was belting out a story about Bareback Jack when I punched the cassette eject button, waiting on traffic headed South on HWY 17 so I could turn into Jack's. Tiff had the window down. The window had blown her hair everywhere. She reached over and grabbed my Mile Zero ball cap. She pulled her hair through the back, making a pony then pushed her bangs up under the front

---

[4] The Most Famous Movie Line and Quotes in Action Films. Access on 01/23/2023 at https://movieweb.com/the-most-famous-movie-lines-and-quotes-in-action-films/#quot-you-39-ve-got-to-ask-yourself-one-question-do-i-feel-lucky-well-do-ya-punk-quot

while looking in the rearview mirror. She turned and smiled at me. I slowly pulled into the gravel parking lot and found a good space up close to the front door. I leaned over and kissed her. Pulling back about six inches from her face. "Are you sure you really want to introduce Amanda to Frankie? Frankie the Freak?"

"She really thinks he's cute! She's from Philly. Went to the same high school, I think. Is there a reason she shouldn't? Is he some major asshole who beats on women or something?" she asked, looking at me for a truthful answer. "You've never told me why the guys refer to him as "the Freak." Is he some kind of pervert?"

I laughed, "No more than any of these other morons! He is actually a model Marine! I have no complaints! When it comes to the Docs, especially Stanley, they're like the damn Three Musketeers, *All for One and One for All.* I have only read about the level of loyalty among them in books. I do not think Hollywood could portray how fierce of loyalty Frankie has for Stanley on the big screen!"

"Why?" Tiff asked, now more intrigued than before.

"A couple of years ago, they were doing a deployment down on the Panama Canal, and Frankie's RAC," noticing the confused look on her face," It's a boat, riverine assault craft - RAC. We were doing night ops; Frankie's RAC collided with what they believe was one of those big, long, banana power boats running dark with no navigation lights. Pretty much cut the RAC in half.

Frankie hit his head on the gunwale of the boat. Knocked him out cold. He fell overboard. He probably would have drowned if Stanley had not shucked his gear, jumped off the stern of his RAC and swam to where he saw Frankie go under. Stanley kept diving till he found him and brought him to the surface. They both ended up spending a couple of days in the sick bay getting IV antibiotics for whatever was in that nasty ass canal water. Stanley received the Navy-Marine Corps Medal. Frankie, he swore a blood oath or some shit to be his eternal bodyguard. I feel sorry for the moron who starts anything with Stanley or the rest of the Docs. *All for One and One for All.* Marine Corps ethos at its finest!" I said, unbuckling my seat belt and getting ready to get out.

Putting her hand on my shoulder, she said, "You still haven't told me why they call him the Freak."

"They started calling him the Freak when we were in Palma de Mallorca, Majorca, Spain. It's an island in the Mediterranean. It is gorgeous, and the beaches… Let's just say for a bunch of damn prepubescent Marines and Sailors. There not a set of woodpecker lips tough enough to crack the wood on any of those soldiers standing at attention the moment they saw their first European beach! Most were too damn embarrassed to go out on the beaches wearing shorts, much less do any sunbathing. Way too much tent pitching going on if you know what I mean."

Picturing the image in her head and trying not to laugh aloud, Tiff said, "I can only imagine."

"Well, Frankie disappeared into the beach bathhouse while the lot of them were standing there drooling. He exited wearing only his Aviators, green jungle boots, and a damn green wool sock as sunblock." I turned my head slightly over my right shoulder as I opened my truck door and started to get out. I wanted to see the look on her face.

She was taking a drink of her travel glass of wine and snorted it. She turned and looked at me. I could tell by the look she had a whole new picture of Frankie now. The stories she had heard over the years, well, now they were starting to make some sense. She started laughing as she jumped out of the truck. She walked around the truck, meeting me at the door, "Amanda is going to love him, I think she's kind of a freak herself!"

"Well then. To Frankie and Amanda!" as I opened the door for Tiff.

Walking past me, she leaned over and whispered, "To Amanda and Frankie!"

As we walked in, I looked around to see who was there. Little Joe was delivering food, and Frankie was enthralled in a conversation Stanley was having with a couple of guys I'd never seen before, surrounded by a couple of the other Docs and a couple of Marines. Tiff headed to the lady's room, and I made my way to the bar. "Hey Senior! How the hell are you, brother?" I asked and arranged three of the good bar stools with backs so Tiff, Amanda, and I could sit at the bar together when she got here.

"Evening, Mike. That Tiff I just saw headed to the lady's room?" Senior asked as he wiped down the bar in front of me, then flopped down a coaster.

"Yeah, we are meeting one of her friends, Amanda, here tonight. She wants to meet Frankie," making a pointing movement with my head over my left shoulder.

Laughing, Senior says, "What she got against this poor girl? Couple Shiners for the two of you?"

"I know, right!" I laughed as well, saying, "Two pints will be perfect till she gets here. What's Doc got going on over there? Looks like he has an audience. He recruiting for a new movie?"

"You're never going to let him live that shit down, are you!" as he poured two Shiners, making a statement more than a question.

"Never! That was some funny shit. You could have started a 14-gauge IV on the veins on Sox's forehead that day! Lance Corporal Turd, Corporal Glass, and I sat in the truck, drank a couple of 12-packs, and laughed our asses off."

"Hi, Tiff," Senior said as he came around the bar to give her a hug.

"Hey Senior! Good to see you," hugging him. "When are you going to come to the house and eat with us?"

"How about you guys bring the kids Sunday, and we'll take the Lady Ashley out and cook on her while cruising the coastline?" looking at me.

"Whatever the lady wants, the lady gets Jack," I said, trying my best not to sound like a sarcastic prick. Well, more than normal!

Tiff looked over at me, then turned back towards Senior, "Sounds amazing, Jack. Looking forward to it."

"Settled! Now, Tiff, you have to tell me what this friend of yours, Amanda, did to you that was so bad you insist on setting her up with Lance Corporal Frankie the Freak?" Senior asked as he walked back around the bar.

"Both of you, Stop it! Now! Before she gets here," she said, glaring at both of us as she sat down beside me. "What's going on over there?" she said, nudging her head towards the gaggle of people surrounding Doc Stanley.

"Well, those two sitting in the booth are Rob and John. From what I've seen tonight, Rob is an illustrator, basically a cartoonist. A damn good one at that! John is an author. Fancies himself a humorist," obviously seeing the look on my face. "You heard me right – a humorist. He wants to be this century's Mark Twain. They're on a walkabout looking for humorous stories they can write and draw about that captures the side of life most Americans never see, nor would they believe from a conversationalist."

"You're fucking shitting me, right, Senior? They are talking to Stanley and Frankie about humorous stories?" looking at Senior, then turning towards the group around Stanley.

"I told them this place had more *sea stories* than they had time to write about," Senior said as he turned and headed towards the kitchen.

"Mike, don't!" Tiff said as I stood up. She already knew what I was thinking before I even did.

"They want sea stories; I know the one that they can't pass up!" I said, then began to chuckle with a devilish grin on my face.

"Okay, but as soon as Amanda gets here, you better come back over here with Frankie in tow. You hear me!" giving me a look like I was about to pay dearly if I screwed up her night.

"Yes, Ma'am!" I grabbed my beer and started walking towards the table.

"Hey Staff Sergeant," Frankie said as he stood up. Stanley stopped talking and turned and gave me a look...that look of... "Fuck, why did it have to be him?!"

"Frankie, Doc, how are you boys doing?" I asked.

"Great Staff Sergeant," they both said.

"Staff Sergeant, this is Senior's friends, John and Rob. They're writing a book. Guys, this is Staff Sergeant Hart," HM3 Billy Halbecker said as I reached out to shake their hands.

"Nice to meet you guys! Senior was just telling me about the two of you and your mission! Sounds pretty damn cool. Can I see any of your drawings?" I asked Rob.

Showing me the few he had already drawn. "Damn, you're *good*, Rob!" I explained, truly impressed with his work.

"How about you tell us a *sea story,* Staff Sergeant?" John asked as he turned sideways in the booth.

"You don't want to really hear anything from me," hoping they would not take "No" so easy.

"Come on, Staff Sergeant. You've been in the Corps a long, damn time. Surely you have a good sea story or two to tell us," goaded Halbecker.

"Well, if you insist! John and Rob, you probably didn't know it, but you've been sitting here talking to a world-famous action hero!"

I could feel Stanley burning holes through me.

"Really, Staff Sergeant? Sox won't let the shit go, and now you!" Stanley said as he got up and started towards the back.

"Where are you going?" Rob asked.

"To take a piss," Stanely said as he walked past me. "You wanna come to hold it for me?" giving me that "Fuck you" look. I just smiled back.

"Sit, Staff Sergeant. Please, have a seat!" John offered.

"Thank you! Well, this is pretty damn funny, and it happened last month...."

0720 Friday, August 20th,
A month ago
HQBN 2nD MARDIV
Camp Lejeune, NC

The air was thick, humid, and muggy. I could taste the salt in the air. The smell of the brackish water of the New River tributaries, the smell of rotting decay was pungent. It was overwhelming this morning. I began to sweat immediately. Stepping out of my truck, my inner voice failed me as I expressed my thoughts out loud across the parking lot. "Damn, I hate August in North Carolina!" echoed.

I looked across the lot to my right, I could see the flagpole standing alone in front of Building 2, rising above the tree line in the roundabout on Holcomb Blvd. The flag seemed helpless and motionless, gravity pulling her toward the ground. There was no evidence of movement. No wind. No chance of any relief. Relief from the heat and humidity – not today, anyway. It was the third Friday of the month, on the first and third Friday of every month, rain or shine, at 0530, on the 2nd MARDIV Parade Field, we formed up for Battalion PT. Today, we had a four-mile battalion run led by the XO, Major Fox, and the Division Surgeon, Captain Walton. The Captain, looks old and frail, but don't let looks deceive you. Under his baggy set of utilities is one hard motherfucker! But it's funny how the CO never seems to attend any Battalion PT sessions. I guess that's one of the perks of having a 'bird' on your collar. Not my circus… not my monkeys… not my problem! That's what I keep telling myself: six years, five days, and a wake-up!

I started walking across the parking lot toward the office with a coffee mug in hand, a spit-shined pair of jungle boots slung around my neck, and a clean pair of starched utilities hanging over my shoulder. Mental note to self, make sure I compliment Jen the next time I drop off my laundry to tell her how good a job she does! I don't know what they use at Saigon Sams to starch their clothes, but I am pretty damn sure these utilities could stand at attention on their own!

Before crossing Julian C. Smith Street and heading into the office, I stopped to check for traffic. Damn sure do not want to get run the fuck over by some PFC Smuckately driving a 5-ton truck. I don't trust these knuckleheads to yield to pedestrians. I looked right…, clear, nothing coming, but off to my left…

I could hear the sound of clapping hands, and feet in synch, striking the ground in rhythm. I turned my head to the left to see who was coming down the road from the north, running, singing a beautiful rhythmic echo and call. The sound of a Marine calling cadence, followed by a company of Marines sounding off in unison, a guidon bouncing with every step, I closed my eyes...

"Lo right, a lo righty a lay o"
" lo right, a lefty righty a lo"

" lo right, a lo righty a lay o"

" lo right, a lefty righty a lay lo"'

" Oh yeah!"

"Oh yeah"

"Sound Off!

"Sound Off!"

"Here we go!"

"Here we go"

" A little run!"

" A little run"

"Just for Fun!"

"Just for Fun!"

"A mile one!

"A mile one"

"A just for fun!"

"A just for Fun"

Then, just as fast as they came up over the rise in the road, they were fading south down towards French Creek, the sound of the cadence still echoing in my head, *A two mile, A give me more,* and for a moment I was back on the drill field.

I walked into the office, noticing I had beat Lance Corporal Blevins, aka Lance Corporal Turd, into the office again this morning. That made me smile. I love giving that shit bird hell. I am unsure what I did to deserve a damn "winger" in my shop, but

I must have done something horrible in my past life! I asked for an 0311 and I got Blevins. Looking towards the heavens, *please, Chesty, give me strength.*

I quickly changed into my utilities, sat at my desk, and started looking at the pile of paperwork which seemed to have accumulated on my desk while I was on leave for the last week. I asked myself, "What in the hell did Lance Corporal Turd do last week? Anything?" From the looks of the notes from Top Walsh, *NOTHING* would be the appropriate answer.

"Morning, Staff Sergeant How was your leave?"

I look up and behold Lance Corporal Turd, still in his PT gear, with a 5 o'clock shadow...*I am going to enjoy this*, maybe a little too much, on my first day back. Just as I was about to rip him a new asshole...

"Staff Sergeant Hart, could you come to see me please?" echoed down the hallway from the XO's office.

"Blevins, DO NOT FUCKING GO ANYWHERE, You and me, we're going to talk! And make a new pot of damn coffee!"

"On my way, sir!" I shouted as I got up out of my chair and started toward Major Fox's office while staring at Blevins, making sure he knew I was not happy with him.

As I walked into the major's office, "Sir, you asked for me?" He was not sitting at his desk, he was standing looking out the window, his back towards me. Major Fox was one of the best bosses I've ever had. A Marine's Marine, a true leader! I had served with him when I was a boot sergeant at 2/8. He was our company commander, a damn good one at that!

"How was your leave, Staff Sergeant?" he asked as he turned to face me.

"Amazing, sir! The backwaters west of Islamorada were perfect, clear as glass, and the bone fishing, well, I landed a nice one. And we caught a couple of tarpons, too! One was a little over seventy pounds, on a #12 weight. It was one helluva fight!"

"Glad you had a good break! You deserved it! Captain Walton called me yesterday. He needs to get four, maybe five of his doc's pistol qual'd. At 1300 today I need you to run the pistol range at D-29. Can you make this happen? Gunny Hall has already made all the arrangements for the range and the ammo."

"Absolutely, sir. You know I'll make it happen. Anything else, sir?"

"That's it, Mike. If you have any issues, you know how to reach me." He then sat back down at his desk.

"Yes, sir!" I did an about-face, left the major's office, and walked back into mine as Blevins starts mouthing...

"What the fuck! Why do the docs need pistoled quals?"

"Blevins, I don't fucking know, and I really don't fucking care. It's not my job to care. It's my job to make sure it fucking happens! It's your fucking job to get your nasty ass into the proper uniform of the day! Make sure you shave that ugly mug of yours because if I have to remind you, it will be a dry shave with my straight razor. Then get your ass down to the range and ensure it's squared away before the docs are ready to go at 1300. That means the lane is FOD free, targets up. I think you get the picture. Comprende?

"Yeah, I comprende!" as he grabbed his trash behind his desk.

"Now that we understand each other, make sure before you leave, call Corporal Glass and make sure he gets the 9mm ammo and has it there no later than 1245. Oh, and Blevin..."

"What?"

"DO NOT FUCK THIS UP!"

"Yes, Staff Sergeant!" as he turned and made his way towards the head. I walked over to the coffee mess and filled my coffee cup. I guess I better call Doc Sox and Gunny Hall to let them know we are a go.......

0750
HQBN BAS
BLDG 8
Camp Lejune, NC

"Stanley, Phillips, Gilpen, Creager, Halbecker! In my office now!"

"I am busy!" came a shout from the pharmacy.

"Stanley, get your ass in my office now" *Why is he always so damn defiant?*

"This is bullshit. I told Gunny Hall I would get a haircut over the weekend. I am not a fucking Marine! Tired of being fucking treated like I am! I am *too* damn pretty. Hair like this… it has charisma. HM2, the ladies love my mother fuckin' charisma!" As he walked into my office holding more than seven inches of hair in his hands.

"Stanley, what the fuck are you talking about?"

"You're not going to chew my ass about my hair?" dropping the hand of hair. By the look on his face, he knew he had screwed the pooch and had just thrown himself under the bus.

"Well, now that you've brought it to my attention, I want to see a fresh haircut by the end of the day!" *Somedays, I wonder how that boy finds his way to the damn chow hall.*

"What! This is bullshit, HM2! Oppressive bullshit!" throwing a tantrum, all 5'2" of his dumb ass, like a toddler. Looking straight at him, "Stanley, you're one word away from something oppressive! You understand me?" Stanley stops his act, shakes his head yes, and stands still for the first time, maybe ever.

"Now that we are finished with HN Stanley's daily urinary Olympics, Phillips, go to the motor pool, check out the hummer, and meet the rest of your knuckleheads at the armory. Check out your pistols. Be there at 1215 sharp! DO NOT BE LATE! Then meet Staff Sergeant Hart at the D-29 pistol range so you can finally get your pistol qualifications completed. All of you. That means

Doc is issued a weapon!

you, too, Charisma BOY. Ride in the ambulance. DO NOT TRANSPORT your government-issued weapons in your POVS!"

"Do you understand me?" Looking at each of them to make sure they understood me, I said, "Shake your head yes."

All five shook their heads in acknowledgment. "Chief Folley said nobody goes home till EVERY SINGLE ONE OF YOU have qual, not familiarized, qual'd. Got it?"

As the other three nodded yes, Stanley stepped forward, placing his hand on my desk and leaning over it, "HM2, I've got important plans! I am heading down to Wrightsville Beach for a fun weekend - sun, brews, boozes, broads, and college babes. Lance Corporal Frankie the Freak and me. We are spreading some of this *Texas* charm, and you know the ladies just can't refuse me when it starts to ooze out! More importantly, tomorrow, I've got something really important to do! Something that's got nothing to do with Uncle Sam's Misguided Morons or haze gray and underway!"

Pushing my chair back away from my desk, "Stanley, do you think Chief Folley gives a flying fuck about your *important* plans?"

Taking a step back, he muttered, "No!"

Standing up and pointing towards the door. "So, if you want to see the beach in this lifetime, get a fucking haircut and be at the armory at 1215! In the meantime, a bunch of sick Marines need to be seen this morning."

"Fine! They're just a bunch of nonhackers with the Budweiser flu! The geniuses decided to get a pony keg last night while they were field daying the barracks. When I left for Jack's, they were doing keg stands!" He snaps to attention, clicking the heels of his boots together, knowingly being a defiant little smart-ass till the end.

"Stanley, what did I do to deserve you? It doesn't matter if they all have the clap and syphilis. It's your job to fix them, so fix them! Now get out of my fucking office!"

"Aye, Aye HM2," as he rendered a piss poor hand salute, did an about-face, and sarcastically marched out of my office followed by the other four.

"Fuck you too, Stanley!" I said while shaking my head as I sat back down in my chair.

Damn, someday I will strangle that little fucker and feed him to the alligators in the New River tributaries! Been asked and reprimanded more than once for allowing Stanley's lack of military bearing to continue "unchecked." Stanley is the worst garrison sailor I have ever known, but the damn Marines love him! Why? Because they know when the shit goes south, and everyone else has left their broken asses to die, Stanley is the only son-of-a-bitch stupid enough, excuse me, the only one brave enough, to walk, run and/or crawl through hell to make sure they make it home one way or the other, or he is going to die trying.

1300
D-29 Pistol Range
Camp Lejeune, NC

"All right, guys, let's gather around for a quick safety brief. My name is Staff Sergeant Hart, and this is Corporal Glass. We are your Range Safety Officers. To my right is Lance Corporal Blevins. He is here to assist you, gentleman, to make sure your time here with us today on Range D-29 is flawless and everyone goes home at the end of the day! Before we get started, does anyone have questions?"

"Yeah, Staff Sergeant, how long do you think this will take?" asked HN Stanley.

"Doc, if everything goes as it should, we should be packed up and out of here NLT 1530."

"Sweet! I gotta some place to be tonight," he said, smiling smugly with his arms crossed.

"Well, then, let's get to it. Here are the safety Rules:

1) Your four safety rules are:

    - Treat every weapon as if it was loaded.

    - Never point your weapon at anything you do not intend to shoot.

    - Keep your finger straight and off the trigger until ready to fire.

    - Keep your weapon on safe until you intend to fire.

2) While on the pistol range, all commands will come from the tower or me in this case.

3) All weapons will be pointed down range when loading, unloading, and dry firing.

4) It is the responsibility of all shooters to give the command *Cease Fire* if they see an unsafe condition.... All shooters assume their appropriate lanes."

I watched the four Corpsmen walk to their respective lanes and begin to load their magazines. "Corporal Glass, are you ready?"

"READY," replied Corporal Glass from the right side of the firing line.

"Gentleman, are we ready? Give me a thumbs up. Four thumbs up. We are good to go!"

"*Standing Position, 7 Rounds.*"

"*Load and Lock.*"

"*Ready on the right?*"

"READY," echoed Corporal Glass.

"*Ready on the left?*"

"READY," yelled Lance Corporal Blevins

"*Ready on the firing line.*"

"READY," is replied by all four docs on the firing line.

"*Unlock your weapons.*"

"*Firers, watch your lane.*"

"*You are cleared to engage your targets.*"

You hear the sound of the safeties clicking off. Then …Pop, Pop, Pop, Pop, Pop, Pop, Pop, Pop, Pop.

Looking down the firing line, *What the Fuck? You have to be kidding me.* What in the hell is Stanley doing firing his pistol over his head, one-handed, sideways?

"*Cease Fire! Cease Fire! Cease Fire on the range!*"

WHY DOC ONLY GETS PISTOL QUALIFIED.

"*Are there any alibis?*" My blood began to boil, waiting to ensure no hot rounds were cooking off.

"Clear all weapons!"

"Clear on the right?"

Corporal Glass replied, "CLEAR ON THE RIGHT!"

"Clear on the left?"

"CLEAR ON THE LEFT!" from Lance Corporal Blevins.

"The firing line is clear." *I am going to kill that mother fucker! So help me, God!*

"Firers, place your weapons on the stand with slides locked to the rear."

"All firers, step back five steps from the stand!" *What the fuck was that shit?*

"Stanley!" and just like that, I am back on the drill field. The knife hand is deployed.

"Stanley, what in the name of the Virgin Mary, Mother of Jesus H. Christ, what was that bullshit?" as the other three corpsmen step back a couple of paces, leaving Stanley to face my wrath on his own.

"Could you please be more specific, Staff Sergeant?" as he looked around to see where the other three had gone.

"Stanley, do not fuck with me! You know exactly what the fuck I am talking about! What kind of bullshit shooting stance was that I just saw you doing! You think you're in the 'hood, doc?" I saw the tan Iroc -Z pull into the parking lot to my left out of the corner of my eye. This *was about to get primitive.*

"Staff Sergeant Hart, something wrong?" HM2 Sox asks as he walks ups.

"Wrong, Doc? Yeah, there are all kinds of wrongs going on here! HN Stanley has decided to fuck up my entire afternoon!"

"How so?" asked HM2 Sox, turning and staring at Stanley.

"For some reason, HN Stanley thinks my pistol range is the 'hood! He thinks his government-issued 9mm Beretta is a Saturday Night Special cap gun. For some reason known only to him and God the Almighty, he believes in that squid brain of his it is okay to fire his pistol, not only one-handed but above his head - perpendicular to the deck!"

"Staff Sgt, I promise you, I will unfuck this situation! Right fucking now!" as he turns towards Stanley. "What the fuck are you thinking?"

Standing firm, all 5'2" of him, he announced, "I was practicing."

I'm pretty sure Sox was trying not to wrap his hands around Stanley's throat. "Practicing? Practicing for what?"

"My movie audition, HM2!"

Through clenched teeth, "A fucking movie audition?"

"It's tomorrow. Remember? I told you I have some really important plans in Wilmington tomorrow. It's a movie audition!" Standing toe to toe, towering over him, looking down, square into his eyes, "A fucking movie audition?"

"Pretty cool, idn'it. I am going to be the next mother fucking Chuck Norris, baby!"

As the veins in HM2's head began to bulge out of his head, I was doing my best not to laugh my ass off. I could see Corporal Glass and Blevins were enjoying this as much as I was.

"All of you! On your backs, now," and they knew the drill. "Six fucking inches! Hold 'em." He turns to me and shakes his head as a gesture of embarrassment, and *I am sorry*. Lance Corporal Blevins, Corporal Glass, and I started policing brass. We knew those five unlucky bastards would not be in any shape to do anything when Doc Sox got done with them. Most people would stop the extracurricular exercise when one of them blew their lunch. Sox is a different breed. He is one hardcore MF who, at a minimum, won't stop till they all spilled their guts and, more likely than not, won't stop till one of them passes out. The really fucked up part is that crazy bastard is on the ground right beside them, going one-for-one. Fuck that shit!

As I walked back to the firing line, I heard, "Movie audition, huh, Stanley? You're going to be a mother fucking action hero! Well, you're going to need to be strong! You'll need some mother fucking six-pack abs, and guess what, HN Stanley? I will help you with that! Six inches! On my count. Flutter kicks. One, two, three, One. One, two, three, Two, One......"

The entire bar gathered around Staff Sgt Hart. Everyone was laughing hysterically, "Did that really happen, Tobey?" Rob asked. "Like this?" as he stopped and looked up from his drawing. Holding it up for everyone to see.

Looking at me, Stanley smiled, lifting his beer, "Maybe. I have to say, to hear you tell it, Staff Sergeant. That was some funny shit! See guys, I told you people wouldn't believe the shit that happens when you're in the military! It's more stupid shit like this than the blood and guts bull shit."

From the bar, the ship bell rang *Ding, Ding, Ding.*

"Who wants another round?" pointing to the huge ass plaque on the wall behind the bar, "Don't forget Rule No.6, keys in the jar, bring me your glasses...

Limousines, Lifers Juice, Coffee Mugs, and Phantom Shitters...

"When my blood runs black as the moonless night, and my heartbeat sounds as the Warriors march, only then may you say, I've had enough coffee."

– Anonymous

0015
Thursday
Jack's BAS Bar & Grill
Hwy 17
Jacksonville, NC

The bar was emptying out. I believe Amanda and Frankie hit it off. Time will tell! Stanley, Gilpen, Creager, Halbecker, Glass, and Gilbey had made their way outside, leaning on each other. *All for One and One for All...* They loaded up into Jack's Long Black Ambulance, helping pour the two boots into the back seat. She's my 1980 midnight black Cadillac Fleetwood limousine I keep at the bar to keep my Marines and Corpsmen safe. With Jimmy "Smitty" Smith behind the wheel, Harley "Bob Marley", and the Cookie Monster riding shotgun playing ambulance, they make a right onto HWY 17, then a right at the Kettle. They were headed northeast up HWY 24 back towards Main Side to the barracks with the last of the heroes. Gotta feeling a few of those boys, especially Stanley and Gilbey, will be hurting come 0530 battalion PT in the morning.

Every time I watch them drive off, I smile and know the money I spend to maintain my stupid limousine business license, the insurance, and all the other BS that goes along with it is worth every penny. When I was a boot, my first CO, a Vietnam Vet - Lieutenant Colonel Green, he was the real deal, not like today's want-to-be warrior kings who dream and pray for combat. He knew firsthand the horrors of war. He didn't pray for war. He prayed for peace. He would tell you so every time he stood in front of the battalion. The paradox was he also knew evil was standing on the doorstep - our doorstep. He knew all too well there is always someone with a chip on their proverbial shoulder out there in the lurch, waiting to hurt you. Waiting, watching for just the right moment. The moment you let your guard down, they will attack – when you are most vulnerable. That is why *we train* and *train for war*, *all day*, *every day,* he would say.

Lieutenant Colonel Green also strongly believed in protecting his warriors, *all day*, *every day* as well, especially from themselves! He had a laminated business card he would personally hand to every member on the first day you checked onboard. It made you feel you were part of something bigger from day one. On the front, it had his name, rank, and unit info, and on the back was a set of directions for a taxi driver. He knew Marines and Sailors were going to drink. No orders, no amount of preaching, nothing was going to stop that. It was just a fact. Hell, the damn United States Marine Corps was contrived by a bunch of drunken fighting men in a bar called Tun's Tavern in Philadelphia, Pennsylvania, in 1775. Nothing has changed in 200-plus years. So, to help counteract drinking and driving, to decrease the risk of his warriors dying needlessly in a dumbass car wreck, not on a battlefield in some faraway country like Marines are meant to do, which is their God-given destiny to do - he instigated the *No Question* program. Anytime one of his warriors was drinking out on the town and didn't have a DD. They would just present the business card to the taxi driver, who would take them back to the barracks. The driver would give the card to the Officer of the Day – the OOD or the Staff Duty Officer, who would pay the taxi fare out of the petty cash coffer, *no questions asked.* You had 30 days to repay the money. Now if you got caught drinking and driving, the old man was going to have your ass! Guaranteed to take a stripe, take half a month's pay for two months, and be restricted to barracks for two months. For the married guys, it fucking sucked. It was a career-ending move and often a marriage-ending one, too!

I tried to carry on a similar tradition with my sailors throughout my career. After I got out and opened this place, I decided I was not going to contribute to one of these morons ending their careers, or worse, ending their lives or someone else's! So, I bought *Black Betty*, and named her after Ram Jam's 1977 song. Got her from a private security company owned by my old Marine

Recon buddy, Jake Owens. Black Betty may look all sweet and pretty on the outside, but she ain't what she seems. She has bulletproof windows, steel-reinforced passenger area, and Kevlar-reinforced tires, and the V8 is pullin' close to 250 horses. She'll tac out the speedometer at 120 plus. It's white knuckle, crazy, damn scary driving! Why do I need that kind of car to haul around a bunch of drunk Marines and Sailors? I don't, but she does generate a lot of conversation. She's a mouthpiece. People appreciate the service and keep coming back! My Rules are ethos, and Marines live by their ethos They will spend their money in establishments with similar beliefs. Some say it makes good business sense, and maybe it does or at least, to me… it's just the right thing to do, nothing more, nothing less!

Making my way back inside, Coop's asleep in front of the jukebox, and the two new recruits look like they are still hard at it. If John is half the writer Rob is a cartoonist, I see these boys having a new full-time occupation in the near future!

"Hey boys, can I get you anything else," I ask as I walk up to their booth. I can't help but look at the drawing laid out on the table. "Rob, do you mind if I look at some of those?" pointing to the drawing on the table.

"Absolutely not, Jack! And thank you!" Rob said as he pushed his glasses up on his nose again.

"For what?" taking the stack of drawings from him.

"For this opportunity!" lifting up his hands like Brother Ray on the pulpit, simultaneously looking around. "We've never heard more funny shit anywhere than we have tonight! I can't believe some of these damn sea stories! Are these guys for fucking real? Or are they just bullshitting us?" John asked me as he put down his pencil, then took one of the mugs of coffee Little Joe just brought the three of us.

"¡Gracias, amigo!" lifting my cup up to thank him.

"That damn down-island blend coffee makes the best lifer's juice you'll ever drink anywhere, just don't ask him how he makes it," shaking my head back and forth like I was saying no.

"Lifer's juice?"

"That's what you call coffee," I said.

"Why's that, Jack?" John asked before picking up the mug and taking a sip of the coffee. Before I could answer, he said, "Damn, Little Joe, this, this good, really good."

"Tanks, man. Mi hope yuh wudda like it," with his huge grin, so large you could see all his white teeth gleaming. "Betta get back an' finish cleaning di kitchen suh mi cya ketch sum sleep." Little Joe Banks, all 5'3" and a buck and a quarter, was once one hardcore, bled Marine Corps green Master Gunnery Sergeant. "Master Guns" Joseph A. Banks, originally from Coral Bay, St. John, U.S. Virgin Island. Only a handful of people still know that about Little Joe. Looking at him, you would not know he's pushing 75. Joe served 40 years plus in the Corps. A 1943 Montford Point

Marine. Saw combat as a "stretcher bearer and ammo runner" on Okinawa. Served two tours in Vietnam – wounded once. I was his Corpsman in Beirut. It's a crazy, funny world - the six degrees of Kevin Bacon, especially in the Corps. Turning towards Joe, "Thanks, Joe. Head home when you're ready, and we'll see you tomorrow!" He just waves in acknowledgment as he heads back to the kitchen.

"You can't be promoted to a Chief or Gunnery Sgt if you don't have a coffee cup permanently attached to your hand. It's the lifeblood of the NCO Corps of all the military services. If you want to truly fuck up your day, fuck with the Chief's coffee and see what kinda' hell you end of end up in. Promise you it won't be pretty! You're more likely to have a free pass if you sleep with his wife versus screw with his coffee, or worse yet, his coffee cup. You're going to die a slow, miserable death, no doubt. The worst mistake a new boot officer or enlisted personnel will make early on in their career is listening to some agitator who tells them the best way to get in the Chief's good graces from the start of their new *tour* is to scrub his nasty-ass coffee mug!" I tipped my cup, showing them the years of coffee stains in my cup.

With a semi-disgusted look on his face, "Damn Jack, when was the last time you washed your coffee mug? Man, we'll buy you a new one. That one needs replacing. We'll pick you up one of those new big ones with the lid, won't we, John," Rob offers, looking to John for some help.

"Last time this thing was washed, Noah was Captain of the Ark," I said, laughing. "Coffee cups are like your grandmother's iron skillet; they're seasoned just right! Takes years, and years, and can be fucked up by some moron and a Brillo pad in 30 seconds or less."

Looking at each other, they just kinda' shrugging their shoulders, "If you say so Senior. I hope your tetanus is up to date," Rob said with a smirk on his face.

"So, what happened to *you* after *you* scrubbed your first mug?" John asked.

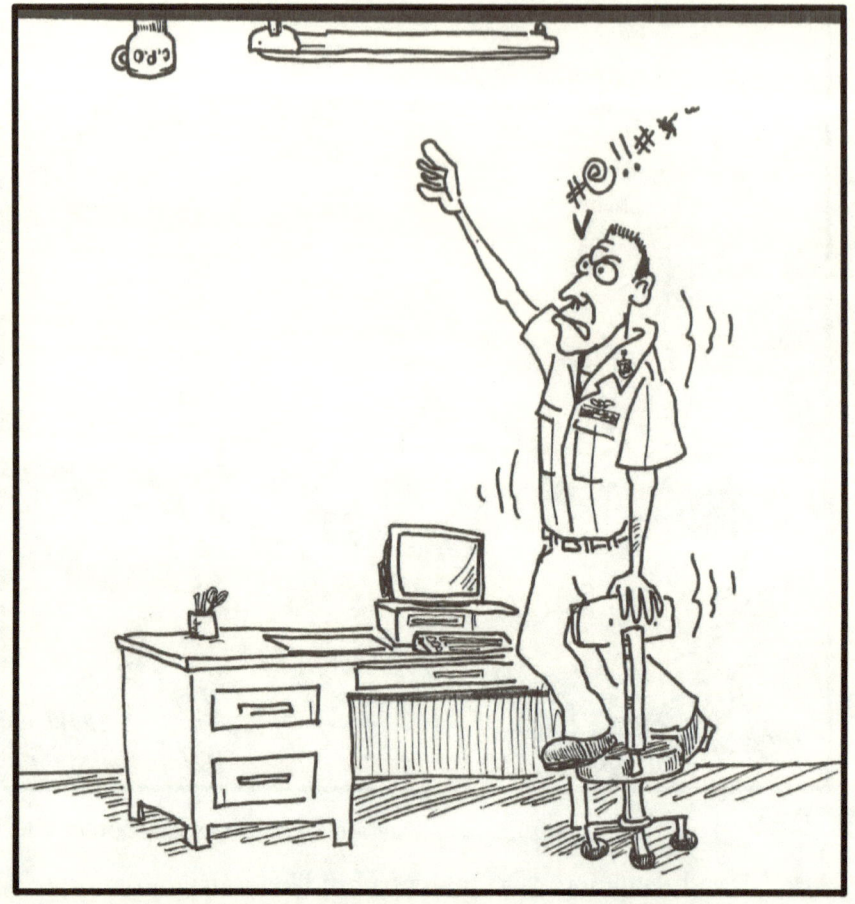

"Me? I was smarter than your average bear. Well, not really, but my old man was blue water Navy, served on a tin can in the South Pacific in '44 and '45. I knew better. However, it didn't stop me from screwing with a Chief or two in my younger days, especially the ones who were just dicks!" followed by a deep breath and a smile.

Breaking open a new drawing pad, "What was the meanest thing you've seen or done?" Rob asks.

"Done and seen, those are two entirely different things! Done - I would come in after hours with a caulking tube of contact cement. The clear rubber kind. I would chalk the shit out of the bottom of the mug, then using a precut painter's pole, I would glue that bitch to the ceiling." Laughing at myself, not realizing I was laughing out loud.

"What's so funny, Jack?"

"Sorry boys, until now, I have never told a soul about me doing that! I always did it alone, with no accomplices, conspirators, and nobody to flip on you. The statute of limitations has expired, and most of those assholes are probably dead. The next morning, I would ensure I was the first in the office. I would get up and be there at NLT 0330 to ensure I removed the pole. It was always a shitstorm afterward for everyone, I mean everyone! That is one of the reasons I never said a word. The Chief would ALWAYS lose their shit. You could hear them for miles in any direction."

"That's some demented psychological deviant warfare taking place there, Jack," John said.

"Demented? That my young friend is deviant but not demented! The phantom shitter, now those SOBs are some demented, deviant little fucks, and if I ever find out who they are, I promise you, the statute of limitations *HAVE NOT* run out on their dumb asses." *Thinking about them still irritates the living shit out of me!*

"What do you mean, Jack?" John asked, with piqued curiosity, obviously due to the irritation the subjects still conjugate within me.

"There is a subset of depraved, demented individuals who desecrate the uniform they wear and fail to honor by getting their little, shriveled peanut jollies off by shitting in people's coffee cups. They somehow think it is funny. They cop-a-squat over the mug, squeeze one off, then transport it back to the owner's desk, leaving it for someone to find." Shaking my head, back-and-forth no, still in disbelief people do this kind of shit!

In disbelief, Rob looked up from his drawings, "Someone took a shit in your coffee mug, Jack? What the hell did they believe you did to them?"

"Honestly, it never happened to me personally. I knew of some guys it did happen to. They were asses, usually, but NO coffee mug deserves that kinda' disrespect! Ever! But the *Phantom Shitter*. What I despise is the fucking asshat who likes to take a shit in the water bull." Obviously, from the looks on their faces, they have no idea what a water bull is.

"Water bull?" I asked, but neither made any kind of gesture of acknowledgment.

"It's usually a 300–500-gallon water trailer used to transport potable drinking water around while you are in the field," I said.

THE PHANTOM SHITTER!

Now they both have disgusted looks on their faces, almost in unison, "Someone shit in your drinking water?"

"Exactly! Fucking disgusting! It was a Preventive Med problem! One fucking wise guy and the entire unit is shittin' their brains out, literally. Had it happen on more than one occasion. It brings the entire unit to its knees, and whatever the operation is, to a grinding halt. Still pisses me off every time I think about it." I said with a hint of disdain in my voice.

"How do you know that it was, a phantom shitter?" Rob asked while he pushed his glasses back up on his face again.

"We check the water several times a day, so every morning, you check it, and then you'll have fecal material... Anyway, people do some really messed up shit to get out of training or operating!"

Having been a long day, it was beginning to wear on me, I stood up then said, "Boys, it's getting late, almost zero-one. The pups and I need to finish shutting up the place. Are you boys coming back tomorrow for another round?" I asked, already knowing the answer.

They both looked at each other, smiled, then turned and looked up at me, "Hell yeah, Senior!"

"Outstanding! Little Joe will be here by 1500ish, and I'll be in and out, but for sure not later than 1700."

The boys packed up their gear, and I walked them to the front door, said goodnight, and finished locking up. I wonder what tomorrow holds in store...

Hard Chargers, Ball Busters, and Two Pink Lines

1945
Friday
Jack's BAS Bar & Grill
Hwy 17
Jacksonville, NC

On the radio, Danny Joe Brown and the rest of Molly Hatchet were singing about pulling themselves out of bed, putting on their walking shoes, and the dreams they'll never see as I pulled into Jack's. Something about rolling down an open highway at 70 mph, wind in the face, and some good Southern rock blaring on the radio helps rejuvenate the soul and replenish the energy that the green weenie sucked out of you during the work week!

From the looks of the parking, the E-4 mafia underground got the word out to powers that be Senior requested our presence tonight. It's nice Senior made a spot for bike parking right by the front door. I pulled up and back into the spot, put the kickstand down, and killed it as Danny finished singing about coming down from the hilltop and getting back in the race!

There were a couple of guys standing outside the door smoking cigars. I recognized Stanley's sidekick, Lance Corporal Frankie the Freak. If he is here, Stanley can't be too far! Those two are like the Lone Ranger and Tonto. I am not sure which one is which!

"Hey Phillips, sweet ride! I love the hunter green and black! It's sharp! When did you get that?"

"Thanks, Frankie! It finally got delivered last month," I said as I removed my gloves and helmet.

"Where did you get it?" Frankie asked.

"I bought it through the MWR in Rota when we did our washdown before we came home. It took damn near a year for it to get delivered, but the price was about one-third less than if I bought it here," I said.

"Damn! That's sweet, brother!" Frankie said.

"What's going on in there tonight?" I asked, pointing towards the front door.

"Lies, tall tales, and sea stories - watered down by beer, fueled by liquor and egos," replied Frankie after he blew a smoke ring in the air.

"So, you're telling me the bullshit is pretty thick in there tonight?" I asked, shaking my head, and chuckled to myself.

"Brother, thick is an understatement!" Frankie said.

I laughed and made my way toward the door.

As I walked in, Senior was behind the bar, and there was a crowd around a table of Corpsmen. I made my way to the bar as Harley "Bob Marley" ran up and jumped up on my leg. I reached down and picked him up.

"Hey buddy, how are you?" I asked him as I rubbed his head behind his ears. He leaned his head over on me like he was giving me a hug. I've never had a dog who gives hugs!

As I walked up to the bar, still cradling Harley, I hollered at Senior, "Hey, Senior, I think "Bob Marley's" been spending too much time with Little Joe."

Senior turned around and looked at me and started laughing. "Phillips, you might be right. What's a dog to do? Are you jealous? Don't you wish you had Harley's life?"

"Maybe I am, Senior. Maybe I am. How about a Yellow Jacket, please, kind sir? And before you ask. Yes, I am on two wheels and only drinking this one beer!" I said.

"I am going to hold you to that!" Senior said as he went behind the bar grabbing a bottle of Colorado Kool-Aid from the cooler.

I put Harley down, and he took off to the next contestant. I stood up and looked over at the guys gathered around Stanley. "What's up with that, Senior? That why you asked us all to come in?"

Senior threw a coaster down and placed my fat bottle of banquet beer on top of it. "Yeah, those two guys in the center are some new friends of mine. They stumbled in here by circumstance. Maybe fate. Who knows, but they seem like pretty good kids trying to make a name for themselves as an author and cartoonist. They're here to tell all you guys' crazy-ass sea stories."

"You mean our crazy-ass sea stories," I said, followed by a grin.

Senior looked at me and said, "Something like that!" then nudged his head towards the group. "Take your dumbass over there and join them!"

I snapped to attention, clicked my heels, and rendered a shitty hand salute, "Aye aye, Senior!" picked up my beer, did an about-face, and headed towards the group. I found an empty chair and pulled it up behind Creager so I could hear what Stanley was rambling about.

Over the next hour or so, I listened to the different guys sway between reminiscing about crazy shit we had done or seen, the stupid shit Marines do, and boasting about our exploits as heartbreakers and life-savers – definitely a lot of good memories shared.

At some point, John, the self-proclaimed humorist, took his turn to ask questions. "Alright guys, Rob and I were talking earlier today, and we were wondering if any of you have served with any females? If so, what's it like? Is that a valid question?"

After he had asked it, there was a moment of silence among us. The silence made him regress back in his chair, with a look on his face that made me think he maybe thought he had overstepped with the question. Then like a gameshow host, on cue, Stanley stepped up and took control of the conversation – I really would not expect anything less.

"Ok, John, before we answer that question, let me ask you a question first. You two have gotta be honest with us, okay?" Stanley asked while looking back and forth between Rob and John, who were shrugging their shoulders and nodding their heads yes.

"Awesome! So, after listening to us so far, and whoever else you guys know from wherever – what do you two think it would be like serving with females on the Green Side?"

They both raised their eyebrows, surprised by the question. After looking at each other, Rob spoke up first. "Dude, I grew up in a house full of women. It was a freaking train wreck in motion. Always one catfight away from a major disaster. There was someone always complaining about something… Who used my hairspray? You're wearing my shirt! Someone used all the hot water, etc."

Then John spoke up, "My opinion is not any different. My mother and sister were deathly afraid of June bugs and spiders. Shit, we couldn't even talk about spiders after 4 pm. If we did, my mom would not – let's say she claimed she could not sleep. She sprayed so much damn bug spray around our house summer, winter – hell, it didn't matter. I am pretty sure I will die in my 50s from some form of carcinogen-related cancer from all the damn pesticide she sprayed. My dad died from what they said was Agent Orange exposure-associated cancer from Vietnam. But if you asked me, it was all those years of my mom spraying for spiders

and June bugs. So, I have a hard time seeing females going out into the field, especially with no curling iron and hairdryer."

For the first time tonight, we were all laughing at something other than our own stupid moronic shit. There was no doubt John believed every word he had just said, and I could actually picture his mother spraying for spiders.

When he finally stopped laughing, Stanley, through a question, pointed at John and Rob, "Boys, you see that blonde back there playing pool in the back?"

Rob spoke up first, "You mean the one with long blonde hair and jean shorts?"

"The one with the arms like we wish we all had!" Frankie chimes in with his unsolicited two cents.

Creager, returning from the head, rejoins us, takes his seat - adds, "That, my friends, is HM2 Stone…better known as HM2 *Stone Cold*, FMSS instructor at Camp Johnson.

Frankie chimed in again, "She's straight biblical boys – Austin 3:16!"

"Austin 3:16? There's no book in the Bible named Austin." John said, looking at Frankie.

Astonished John didn't know the reference regarding Austin 3:16, Frankie started to explain, "Brother, you've never watched WWE Wrestling. That my friend is Stone Cold Steve Austin's signature '*I just whipped your ass!*' quote!"

By the look on his face, John was still not getting it. "Boys, do you remember the other night we talked about the types of Field Med instructors?" Stanley asked.

"Yeah, the ones that were pissed because they felt like their career counselors screwed them," Rob answered.

"No, the other ones. The one that drank the Kool-Aid?" Stanley asked, and they both nodded their heads yes. "HM2 Stone not only drank the damn shit, but she seasons all her food with it like its salt and pepper! She holds the record for the most pull-ups in a 24-hour period." Stopping to make a point, "Yeah, you heard me right, 24 hrs. She runs a sub-6-minute mile, and Frankie was not kidding about kicking your ass!"

Standing up from his chair, "Next time you go to the head, nonchalantly take a look at her. She got a huge ass shiner!" Frankie said.

"She's got a black eye? Why?" John asked.

"Like I said, Austin 3:16. She's involved in that mix-martial arts cage match fighting bullshit! Stanley and I have seen her fight a couple of times; to say the least, she is absolutely brutal in the octagon!" Frankie proclaimed.

Stanley takes over the conversation again, "Let's just say, any female who has had HM2 Stone as their instructor can stand on their own two feet in about any environment the big green weenie is going to throw at them."

Rob puts down his pencil, looks up from his sketchbook, and looks straight at Stanley, "So what are you telling us, Tobey, is that you guys haven't had any issues with females while on the Green Side?"

"Nope, hold them horses right there, Hoss. That's not what I said at all, Rob," Stanley said with both hands in the air like a stop sign. "Why don't we ask Phillips over there about his first day at Headquarters Battalion."

I had been idly sitting there throughout the evening, just listening, until now. Now Stanley somehow had pulled me into his little dog and pony show, and I could do nothing about it! Except for firing back insults – "Fuck you, Stanley!"

"Easy there, Hoss. You gotta' admit it was funny as hell!" Stanley replied to my comeback.

He was not wrong, but he was wrong for shoving me in front of that moving bus just now. "It was that!" I replied.

Rob spoke up, "OK, no inside jokes here. That's the rule, so spill it. We'll be the judge about whether or not it is funny." Then he cracked a huge ass grin.

"Fine, but since I am not drinking tonight, someone is buying my damn dinner!" I grudgingly accepted Stanley's challenge.

John said, "Not a problem." Then he stood up, "Hey, Senior," patiently waiting on a reply, "Put Phillip's dinner on our tab." Senior raised his hand to acknowledge him. He sat back down and looked up at me, "Done. Time to spill the beans!"

I took a drink of my *one* and *only* beer, took a deep breath, and said, "Let's get this train rolling."

1450
Friday - A Few Months Prior
HQBN BAS
BLDG 8
Camp Lejeune, NC

S tanding in the men's head, looking in the mirror, *Alright, J, you have everything? Orders?* Check. *Medical record?* Check? *Gig Line straight?* Good to go. *Let's do this!* I picked up my orders and records and made my way toward the BAS.

"Can I help you, Petty Officer?" asked the HN in *Johnny Cash's* sitting behind the check-in desk.

I must admit, I think Johnny Cash's, the Navy's long-sleeve, winter working uniform, are sharp and unique, but I hate that damn tie. However, I still prefer wearing my Marine Regs. I earned them.

"Petty Officer Phillips, checking on board," I said.

The HN behind the desk stood up with a welcoming smile, stuck out his hand, and then said, "Welcome aboard, HN Tobias Stanley. I just checked in last month myself. Let me show you around. Chief Folley went to the Division Surgeon's Office, but she'll be back soon."

"She?" I questioned.

Rolling his eyes, "Yeah, she! Chief Folley is one of the first Navy female corpsmen assigned to the FMF, and she's a real ball-buster. She's had me stand a full sea bag inspection every day this week!"

With a chuckle, "Hence, the Johnny Cash's?" I asked.

"Yeah, like I said, she's a real ball-buster. But she's a straight shooter. No bullshit. What you see is what you get!" Stanley said. "Stow your gear over here," pointing to an area behind his desk, "until we find you a space."

Nodding my head, "I can handle that. It's a welcomed change from the last fucking Chief I had." The next thirty minutes were spent introducing me to the rest of my new colleagues and showing me around, though there was not much to show. Just a bunch of cubicles made from partitions, the Chief's office, two offices for the two medical officers, two for sick call, the pharmacy, and the supply locker.

When the Chief made it back, our meeting was brief. I was going to be assigned to sick call. Being a full-time provider, working directly for the two medical officers is my dream job. However, I wasn't sure how to take my new Chief. Her utilities were crisp. Her jungle boots were gleaming and well-polished. Her fingernails were well-manicured but not polished. If anything, it was clear. Her frame was tall and thin. Her arms were muscular. She kept in shape. She definitely was not like some of the previous Chiefs I have had.

Sitting with correct posture in her chair, Chief Folley said, "Petty Officer Phillips, we only have one medical officer, Captain

Walton, currently. You'll be working with him, HM3 Creager, and HN Stanley. You'll report to HM2 Frank Sox. You'll see patients every morning Monday-Friday. 0730 - 1600. We man the BAS on Thursday nights till 2100. You know how Marines and field daying usually goes - someone ends up needing sutures."

Knowing her point all too well, I said, "I understand you loud and clear, Chief! Someday I will write a book about all the stupid shit Marines do when they have limited supervision."

Shaking her head back and forth and smiling, "The problem with that, Jay, is even "Hollyweird" would call you a liar."

"You're probably right, Chief."

"Oh, there is one other thing. We have about 200 female Marines and Sailors in the Battalion. How are your OB/GYN assessment skills?" she asked me.

Wide-eyed, like a deer caught in the headlights, I didn't know what to say. That caught me off guard. I had not even thought about that when I requested a transfer to Headquarters Battalion. For the last two years, all I had taken care of was jock-rot-itch, clap-gonorrhea dripping penis, whining, here's some Motrin and foot powder, a shot of Rocephin, crayon-eating swinging-dicks. There are no WMs in a line company.

Leaning forward in my chair slightly, maintaining eye contact, "Chief, I have never treated a female unless you want to count the horses and cows back home before I joined the Navy. Hell, that is why I joined the Navy! I was tired of freezing my ass off helping calve in the middle of the damn winter!" She cracked a smile. A slight one; I know I saw it.

"Petty Officer Phillips, I tell you what. I'll let HM2 Sox know you'll see every female Marine and Sailor who passes

HAZARDOUS DUTY!

through our door seeking treatment for the next two weeks. That should be enough time to sharpen those OB/GYN assessment and treatment skills. Well, enough to get you through what we need here. I suggest you pull out your HM2 advancement material and refresh before Monday."

This can't be that bad, right? "Sounds like a great plan Chief. I will catch up over the weekend and be ready to hit the ground running on Monday," I told her. *It can't be that much different! Seriously, a Marine is a Marine, right?* She is not stupid. She knows I won't look at shit.

She stood up, "I like your attitude, Petty Officer Phillips. If what I heard about you and what I've seen today is what I get out of you, you're going to do well here! It's Friday, and we're down to a skeleton crew. Go ahead and get out of here. We'll see you bright and early Monday morning. Bring your PT gear. We shut the BAS down at 1115 and PT at lunch. Captain Walton is in charge of Monday PT and is a runner - rain or shine!"

Standing up, at attention, "Aye, Aye, Chief. Thank you. See You Monday."

0645
The following Monday
HQBN BAS
BLDG 8
Camp Lejune, NC

I was fifteen minutes early for my first day. I decided to try at least and make an attempt at a good impression. My utilities were sharp, crisp, thin as a wafer, and stiff as a board. Damn, I thought I would have to use a crowbar to pry the legs apart so I could put them on this morning. They are still a little raspy and brash on the thighs, but they'll loosen up after I walk around some this morning. I have to say I spent more time polishing my boots over the weekend than I did prep for OB/GYN. *How hard can it freaking be?*

Looking at my boots. I must say – Damn, *they clean up alright for a worn-out pair of jungles.* They're not reflective like a pair of Coframes - hopefully, the cranky ass First Sergeant Stanley told me about will not give me shit today. Stanley told me he was a *Winger.*

Stanley said the First Sergeant walks around the building with a corn cob up his ass looking for shit to bitch and moan about. He seems to have a hard-on about jungle boots. He believes they should have been retired with the old Marine khaki Summer Service uniforms and Eisenhower Jackets.

The morning moved quickly. First, we had a quick ten-minute, motivational "Let's do this" formation. Then I spent 20 minutes talking with the Medical Officer – Captain Walton. He's a pretty exciting doc. I think I will like working for him.

As I walked out of his office, he asked if we could pray. *Of course, what could hurt, right?* I was unsure what to think when he prayed God lifts my hand to heal the sick and injured Marines we were about to treat. That was something new for me. The first hour consisted of the typical Marine sick call – multiple cases of the Budweiser Flu and the Joe Cuervo associated, "Doc, I don't feel so good this morning. Do you think I could get an IV and a chit restricting me to the barracks," followed by the First Sergeant walking through like a guard on convict row, inciting or instilling fear. I'm not sure exactly which, maybe both. But his presence tended to thin the ranks some.

At 0915, Chief Folley stuck her head in my door and let me know my first female patient had just checked in. She kindly informed everyone during our 0700 formation I would see all the female patients for the next two weeks. She then further suggested they be sure to give me all the support and encouragement I needed to succeed. Which in turn brought a lot of laughing, jeering, and suggestive comments. *Again, how bad can it be? A Marine is Marine – Male, Female...they both bleed red. Electronics over hydraulics! I got this!*

Stanley brought me the patient's record. *She was a 20-year-old Caucasian female. She has no significant past medical history, has four days of nausea and vomiting, and has been unable to eat and keep anything down.* Seems pretty straightforward. Sounds like everyone else I had seen this morning. To tell you the truth, from what I had seen at the Tarheel and Club 108, these female Marines can drink like their male counterparts. As a matter of fact, I have seen many go shot-for-shot and drink them under the table. My clinical gestalt says Budweiser Flu is at the top of my differential diagnosis list.

HM3 Sanderford, the other female Corpsman in the BAS, accompanied me during her physical exam – not going to make that mistake. I had heard horror stories about providers being accused of assault and not having a chaperone to cover your ass in case there are ever any allegations. It's your word against theirs, and you will lose every time. I presented my patient to Captain Walton. I told him her exam was pretty much unremarkable and recommended we tank her up with fluids and Phenergan for her nausea and vomiting.

"When was her last menstrual period?" Captain Walton asked.

Fuck! I did not ask her that question! Never crossed my mind. That is not a standard question I had to ask an infantry Marine. Guess I should have brushed up on my OB/GYN. I apologized and told him I had not asked that question. He then gave me a quick education on why I should always ask that question to every female of childbearing age I treat. He further explained I should order an HCG lab test on every female of childbearing age with XYZ symptoms and if I ever plan to give them medications other than A, B, or C. I thanked him, graciously apologized, and told him I would get that ordered. I followed up with her, and she informed me her aunt was almost two months late. Her aunt? Two months late? Late for what? The euphemisms were lost on me! Then she proceeded to tell me the only reason she came in today was to get a pregnancy test. *Fuck why didn't she just say that?*

I found Sanderford to ask her – one, what the hell is an HCG, and two, how the hell do I go about ordering it? I was not going to give Stanley or Creager any more cannon fodder than they already had by asking them. She said you don't have any kids, do you? I shook my head no. I told her I didn't even have a girlfriend. After she stopped laughing, she graciously explained an HCG test was the lab test for Human Chorionic Gonadotrophin - the two pink line dipstick test to tell you if you're pregnant. I sent the Lance Corporal to Building 65, first floor, to the lab for an HCG and told her to follow up with us after 1300. I asked Sanderson, was that all I had to do? She told me pretty much. *Shit, that's not hard! I got this?*

The rest of my morning rolled along the same. I have two more female patients come through. I presented them to Captain Walton, tanked them up with some normal saline, sent them to Building 65, and told them to return any time after 1300 for their results. My first morning of sick call went pretty damn smoothly! We broke for lunch at 1130. I changed into my PT gear. Captain Walton took us for a nice slow paced 3-mile run. Came back, went by the chow hall, grabbed a quick bite, showered, and was back in the BAS by 1255, ready to see what the rest of my day held.

1315
Monday
HQBN BAS
BLDG 8
Camp Lejeune, NC

"Philips, that Lance Corporal you sent to Building 65 this morning is back for her results," yelled Stanley from the check-in desk.

"Roger, that! Have her take a seat in the waiting area." I replied. I saw her walking to find a seat. She was the only patient we had. As I walked by and headed to the Chief's office, I stopped by and asked her if she was feeling better. She said she was. Said her nausea had subsided. She definitely didn't look so damn ghostly pale. I thought to myself – fluids always cure the BW flu.

I walked into Chief Folley's office to get the results of her HCG, CBC, and BMP results. The one computer we have with a printer was in her office. She showed me how to access the results. We typed in the Lance Corporal's name and DOB, and I'll be damned, she was pregnant! Now what? I knew I should have read that damn study guide!

Chief Folley told me, she must take the printout to the Naval Hospital and go to the OB/GYN clinic. She told me the problem was no longer ours. They will pick up all her care from this point forward. *Really? Sweet!* Why does everybody make such a big deal out of this? It's pretty straightforward. I got this.

I returned to my office and asked the Lance Corporal to follow me. As we walked in, I asked her to have a seat on the exam table. I told her I had got the results of her tests. I told her that her CBC and chemistries were all within normal limits.

"What about my pregnancy test? Did you get those results?" she asked.

"Yes, your HCG was positive. You're pregnant," I told her. What happened next was fucking insane! You just had to be there to understand, honestly. The petite, cute blonde Lance Corporal I had never seen before this morning transformed into Lance Corporal crazy-ass-bitch-from-hell. It was like watching Bruce Banner transform into the Hulk after someone had made him mad.

Her body just clinched up. If her eyes had been lasers, I would have been nothing but smoldering ash.

She screamed "Motherfucker!" at decibels so freaking high, I am surprised the damned windows didn't explode. As she jumped off the table and started kicking the shit out of it!

I got up out of my chair and started towards the door. This crazy chick had lost her mind, and I was looking for an exit! I really should have read that damn study guide. Then she started throwing things off my desk. I was ducking and dodging, but I failed to dodge the flying Merck Manual - a *medical bible* about the size of a dictionary. It caught me square in the nose, which began to bleed immediately.

As I was about to open the door, Sox barged in the door. "What the fuck is going on in here?" he yelled. Between her yelling, the kicking fit, and shit hitting the walls, it didn't take an idiot to figure out shit had gone sideways. Seeing me holding my nose and obviously seeing the blood, he assumed I had done something to her. "What the fuck did you do to her?"

"Nothing, HM2! I just told her that she was pregnant, and she lost her shit. She turned into this instant psycho-bitch," I said in my defense.

Trying to understand what was going on, he asked, "Are you the father?"

"I have never seen this psycho before this morning," I replied.

Lance Corporal Insta-Psycho has run out of things to throw and was done kicking the table. She turned and looked at us as Chief Folley walked into the room. She was standing there with tears streaming down her face. Her make-up was running, leaving streaks. Her perfectly pulled-up shoulder length hair was hanging in her face.

Chief Folley stepped in, "Are you ok?"

"No," she replied.

"Did Petty Officer Phillips hurt you?" Chief Folley asked while looking at me with daggers in her eyes.

She shook her head no, then brushed the hair out of her eye. "No, why would you think that?" she asked.

"Because you screamed 'Motherfucker' loud enough I heard you at the other end of the building, you have kicked the shit out of a defenseless exam table, and someone or something has hit Petty Officer Phillips in the nose," Chief Folley said to her.

"Oh my God, did I do that?" she asked.

Now holding a towel to my face, I nodded my head yes.

With more giant tears running down her face, "Petty Officer Phillips, I am so sorry. I did not mean to hurt you!" Lance Corporal Insta-Psycho said.

"What happened? Why all of this?" Chief Folley asked as she extended both her arms to help visualize her confusion.

"I just found out I am pregnant," Lance Corporal Insta-Psycho said as she sat in my chair. She put her head in her hands and started shaking her head.

"I understand, but that doesn't help me understand all of this," Chief Folley said, confused.

"I was dating a Staff Sergeant who is an instructor at SOI on Camp Johnson. We only slept together one time! One freaking time! Can you believe this shit! One...*Fucking*...Time! One Time! I swear! Two days later, his wife knocked on my barracks door."

Looking up at us, her tears had stopped. But her anger had returned, and with it a sense of calmness about her. "His fucking wife wanted me to know I was sleeping with a married man! I have not seen or talked to that motherfucker in two and a half months. Can you believe this shit? I slept with that worthless motherfucker one time. Told me he was divorced and had a vasectomy. Fuck me!"

At this point, HM3 Sandford stepped in and took over the care of Lance Corporal Insta-Psycho. I am pretty sure she broke my nose with that damn book. The bleeding finally stopped. Ten minutes later, the shiners were beginning to start along with the heckling from the jesters. You can only imagine: "I guess you should have zigged instead of zagged. I should ask her out on a date – crazy looked good on me, etc." ... "Go Fuck yourself, Stanley!" I muttered.

The next thirty minutes were spent cleaning up my exam room. By then, I had raccoon eyes – underneath both eyes were two large, beautiful black-n-blue shiners. What are you going to do?

I had just finished when Stanley let me and everyone in the BAS know my next patient was there to get her lab results. I left my office, and Stanley sat behind the check-in desk, smiling like a Cheshire cat. I asked the Lance Corporal to have a seat in my exam room and went to Chief Folley's office to get her results.

I sat there staring at the screen. You *have to be fucking kidding me*!

"You alright, Phillips?" Chief Folley asked.

"No, not really! This one is pregnant too! What did I do to deserve this? Really?" I said as I stood up.

Chief Folley looked at me, "I would leave your door open and try to be a little more sympathetic."

"Yeah, sympathetic. Right, Chief, on it!" I said as I walked out the door.

The Lance Corporal was sitting on the table as I walked in. I stood up this time and positioned myself between her and the open door. "Lance Corporal, I have your results of HCG, and it was positive. We need to get you over to the Naval Hospital OB/GYN clinic so they can start your prenatal care."

She said absolutely nothing. I mean nothing, not even a sigh. Her face was stone cold as she stood up and walked over to the window. She stood there looking out the window for 30-45 seconds.

"Lance Corporal, are you alright?" I asked her while maintaining my distance.

She turned around, slid down the wall, and started wailing like a baby. She was lying face-first on the floor, a sobbing blob saying over and over, "He doesn't love me anymore."

HM3 Standford heard the commotion and came to my assistance. "What did you say to her, Phillips?" she asked.

"I tried to explain she had a positive HCG, and we would help arrange her prenatal care at the Naval Hospital," I told her.

Sanford started shaking her head as she helped Lance Corporal Wailer up off the floor, who then told us she had just broken up with her boyfriend from back home this past weekend. She didn't know what she was going to do. At some point, thank the Lord, Sanford stepped in to help me finish her care and get her over to the Naval Hospital.

Stanley was kind enough to inform me, "At least this one didn't leave you with any broken bones, lacerations, contusions, hematomas, or other visible injuries, Jay."

"Thanks, Buddy!" as I flew him a double barrel bird. He just laughed and went back to doing nothing at the front desk.

1705
Monday
HQBN BAS
BLDG 8
Camp Lejeune, NC

"Well, Phillips, you have had a helluva first day!" said Chief Folley as she stood in my doorway.

"Chief, it's one I won't forget anytime soon, that's for damn sure!" I replied.

"Why don't you wrap it up and get out of here? Call it a day."

"Aye, Aye, Chief," I replied.

"Phillips."

"Yes, Chief."

"Good job today. Let's try not to break anything tomorrow," she said, then gave me a big grin.

I packed my gear, changed out of my utilities into some PT gear, and headed out the back door to the parking lot to my truck. I was putting my gear in the passenger side when I heard "Petty Officer Phillips." I turned around and saw the Corporal who I had also ordered an HCG early in the day. She had been my last sick call patient of the morning.

"Petty Officer Phillips, I am sorry I am late. I got caught up at work. Is there any chance you could get the results of my pregnancy test from this morning?" she asked.

I instantly got this horrible feeling in my stomach. I felt nauseated. I tried to hide the fear that was welling up inside of me. Every ounce of me was yelling, *just say no.*

"Yeah, come on, follow me," I told her. I shut my truck door and then proceeded back to the BAS. I unlocked the back door and headed in. As we walked past, I noticed Captain Walden was still sitting at his desk reviewing charts. I asked her to sit in my exam room and headed for Chief Folley's office. She was packing up for the day. I told her the Corporal had caught me in the parking lot as I fired the computer back up.

I typed in her name, her DOB, and then went to the Labs section. Instantly, I dropped my head on the desk, making a loud thump. "You've got to be fucking kidding me!" I said as I sat there shaking my head on the desk.

"What's wrong?" Chief Folley asked.

"What's wrong, Chief? She's fucking pregnant, Chief! That's what's wrong!" Instantly, Chief Folley began to laugh. "This is bullshit, Chief! Absolute bullshit!"

Trying but failing to contain her amusement at my expense, "You better go tell her the news. And be sweet, Phillps. Let's try and see if you can get through one patient encounter with having to be rescued! Can you do that?"

"I am not going to do it! You're going to have to go tell her, Chief," I said.

"You've lost your mind, Phillips! You must have got hit harder than we thought this morning! I think you've suffered some type of lame-ass brain injury if you think I am going to do your job!" Chief Folley matter-of-factly put it to me.

"I am not doing it," I replied.

"Phillips, either you get your ass in there and tell her she is fucking pregnant, or I am going have you're as hauled off to the brig for failure to follow a direct order." Her smile had been replaced with the ball busting face Stanley told me about. "Do you understand me?"

I reached over and picked up the phone, and then reached out to give it to her, "Chief, you can send me to CCU. I'll break big rock into little rocks and sand, but I didn't sign up to deal with hormonal Insta-Psycho killer jarheads!"

"Phillips, I never figured you for a pussy. All those exploits I have heard about with the infantry were either fabricated, or your balls have shriveled up and now look like a bunch of grape seeds! No wonder you don't have a damn girlfriend!" Chief Folley said.

Her words diced not only my sense of honor but my manhood too. "Damn, that's some mean, low, uncalled-for, below-the-belt shit right there!" I slammed the phone. "That was wrong, Chief! Just wrong! Don't worry, I got this!" I turned around and printed the results out on the noisy-ass dot matrix printer. I turned and walked past her and out the door towards my exam room. I know I saw her smirk.

I walked into the room. The Corporal was sitting on my stool. I handed her the lab results and took ten paces toward the open door. I saw her reading the results, and then she looked up at me.

"What are you doing?" she asked.

"Did you read the results?" I asked.

"Yes," she replied.

"Do you know what they mean?" I asked.

"Yes, I am pregnant," She replied.

"Are you ok with that?" I asked her.

"I am, yes. My command, I am not so sure about. Why are you acting so freaking strange, Doc?"

Pointing to what now was two black eyes and a swollen nose, "You see this? You're my third positive pregnancy test this afternoon, and no offense, Corporal, but the other two did not handle the result as calmly as you are."

She chuckled, "I heard about this morning. No, me and my husband have been trying for a while now."

I got her finished up and out the door. I was also on my way out when I heard, "Petty Officer Phillips, looks like that went well."

"It did Chief. I'll see you in the morning," I told her.

"See you in the morning, Petty Officer Phillips."

"Did that Lance Corporal Insta-Psycho really break your nose?" John asked.

"She did. That damn book caught me right across the bridge of the nose. I am surprised it didn't slice it open," I said.

"So, what has it been like since?" Rob asked.

"Never had more than one positive HCG in a day! Just normal sick-call stuff. Man, Marines are Marines, male or female - they are all subject to doing stupid shit from time to time. I think it is wired into their DNA," I said.

"What about the Ball-Busting Chief? She still breaking your balls?" John asked.

"Actually, she turned out to be one of the best Chiefs I have ever had. Unfortunately, she just retired two weeks ago. If you guys don't mind, I need to take a head break and get me another beer. You guys need anything?"

Ephesians 5:18: The Padre and the Preacher

2130
Friday
Jack's BAS Bar & Grill
Hwy 17
Jacksonville, NC

When Senior called me this morning asking me to spread the word to the E-4 Mafia about his need for *Sea Stories* this weekend, I first thought he had some promotional gig up his sleeve, trying to pull off some crazy scheme. I didn't know what kinda' hare-brained, off-the-wall scheme he was trying to pull off *this time*. However, the more he talked about it, the more emphatic he became. I knew there was more to the story. I just didn't know what. But, come on, really? What kind of *writer* comes to J-ville, North Carolina, looking for their *golden ticket?* Creager and Gilpen had already talked with Stanley when I spoke with them this morning after sick call, and from the looks of the bar tonight, the E-4 Mafia underground has obviously been hard at work. Leaning with my back against the bar, I looked around, he may not have meant it to be some kinda' gimmick, *but damn Senior, the bar is full tonight, brother.* I have not seen this many Corpsmen in one place since the Corpsman Ball last June.

As I looked around, taking account of everyone I knew, I saw the empty booth in the corner. Well, I should clarify *no one* was sitting there. Couldn't help but smile. The Monster had claimed the northwest corner booth as her own domain. She was curled up, sleeping like a queen on her throne. Someone, most likely Little Joe, had moved her bed off the bar to the booth, and Cooper had found his way up under the table. He was making haste of an enormous ass leg bone. Knowing Little Joe, he brought back a ham hock from somewhere and decided to share it with Cooper. You'll catch a glimpse of Harley's running around here, loving on the ladies, as usual! Stanley swears up and down that Little Joe *slips* him some of his *homemade brownies* – it's the only way that dog can be that damn happy all the damn time! Those dogs are indeed a cornerstone of the bar. So much of the atmosphere around her revolves around man's best friend, and that's what makes this place feel more like a refuge, like home, not just a place you come to in order to escape life. It's not a place to hide in! Those dogs provide so much therapy, a touch of humanity. A piece of home when these guys are missing theirs and needing it most! Senior definitely has created something here that is different for sure!

From behind me I heard "Francis!" I turned around towards the voice calling my name.

"Hey, Senior!" I said, greeting my old mentor, "Looks like the E-4 Mafia spread the word for ya!" Then I started to laugh, extending my arm to shake his hand.

Reaching out, taking my hand with a firm grip in his massive hands, "Yeah, it never ceases to amaze me the depth, the length of effort, and the motivation that junior NCOs will exert to make shit happen *when there is free alcohol involved!* What's your poison tonight, Doc?".

"Think you can give me a better Sunrise in the morning?" I asked with a smirk.

"That I can do! But you're not getting any fucking fresh sliced fruity shit in *your drink* except maybe a lime!" He laughed as he grabbed a bottle of Jose and a glass.

"Fine by me, Senior. You're the chef. I'm just here for the ride! How's the *Sea Story exchange* going?" I asked as I turned and looked over my shoulder at the group surrounding what I assumed were the two guys Senior had told me about.

"Well, I am pretty sure those two are in over their head and have no earthly clue on how to process what they have heard thus far." He finished mixing my Tequila Sunrise and sat it down in front of me on a coaster, "They just keep asking me if these guys are full of shit?"

"Well, I heard Hart told them about our Movie Star last night," looking up at Senior and smiling.

"Fucking Stanley. To hear Hart tell it last night, seriously, that was some funny shit. You can't make that shit up!" Pointing toward the group as he threw his dish towel over his shoulder, "Last night I saw the cartoons Rob sketched, the ones of how he envisioned it taking place. Now that is some funny shit! If John can write half as good as Rob can draw, this book will be some hysterical reading."

From across the bar, "HM2, HM2 Sox," I turned over my left shoulder towards Creager, who was calling me.

"HM2, come over and meet Senior's friends we talked about this morning. The two who are writing the book about Green Side Corpsmen," Creager said, standing and waving me over to the table where the group of Corpsmen was standing.

Making a nudging motion with his head, "Go ahead, I won't let anyone take your leaning post, and I'll have Little Joe throw you a steak on the grill. You good to go with that?" Senior asked, prodding me to join the rest of them.

Grabbing my drink in my left hand, "Fine!" I exclaimed, attempting to present a false pretense of being put out. Turning toward the waiting audience, I started walking toward the three-ring circus. Senior seemed to be the ringmaster, wearing his tall hat and coattails. Pretty sure I was just voluntold to be tonight's juggler, or maybe the jester. It's too soon to tell.

Creager stood beside Senior's friends, "John, Rob. This is HM2 Frank Sox. HM2, this is Seniors buddies, John, who is an author, and Rob, he's a damn good cartoonist."

"That's what I hear," I replied. "Looking forward to seeing what you've thrown together."

They both stand up, each taking their turn shaking my hand. Pushing his glasses up on the bridge of his nose, "It's a pleasure to meet you, HM2. Are you the same HM2 Sox that Staff Sergeant Hart told us about that thrashed the living shit out of Stanley a while back?"

"Well, not sure, thrashing is the appropriate description," looking over at Stanley, then looking back at them, "I like to think of it more as *remedial physical training.*"

"Remedial physical training... I love it! I'll have to remember that." John said as he sat back down. "HM2, do you have any sea stories that you would like to share with us?"

"Me? Sorry guys, this is your show. I am just a tourist here to enjoy the scenery and hang out with my friends!" I told them, not really planning on partaking in the ongoing circus or revival, depending on your point of view.

From behind the bar, I heard a clear statement, "Educate the boys about our other naval brothers in green," Senior yelled. I turned and gave him that understood look that only two old friends know, the one that says *fuck you.* He smiled that huge ass grin of his, "Exactly! That one! Tell them about the Padre and the Preacher." I am now locked into this with no honorable way out. I turned back around.

"Ok, I can do that, I guess," giving in. I took the chair Creager had pulled over for me next to Phillips. "Thanks, brother!

From what Senior tells me, these braggarts have only told you about themselves. I am correct?"

"Not sure what you mean?" John asked.

"Senior was alluding to the fact there is more to the Green Side than just Corpsmen. Granted, we comprise the lion's share of naval personnel assigned to the Corps. However, there are *our real Docs* - the Medical Officers often called the Battalion Surgeons. Don't let the title fool you, though. They're great at what they do, but they're not surgeons. They're usually GMOs, general medical officers, with only a few years under their belt. Still, they will fight like a bull elephant to protect their Corpsmen and Marines." I stopped to take a drink and looked around as more of the Corpsmen began to gather around.

Picking up where I had left off, "There are the few nurses assigned to the FSSG, the dentists, and their dental tech. Still, the ones that have brass balls so damn large they have to carry them in a wheelbarrow are the chaplain and their RPs." The two college boys were keeping up with me pretty well. Still, I saw the blank stare. The one that screams, what the hell is he talking about?

"An RP is a Religious Program Specialist - i.e., a part-time enlisted altar boy and full-time bodyguard... for the Chaplain."

Raising his hand like he was in junior high, Rob politely interjected, "Sorry to interrupt, HM2 Sox... but why do chaplains need bodyguards? They're men of God, right? They shouldn't need bodyguards."

Turning and looking at Rob, "Don't apologize, brother, and it's Frank," I replied.

"You ever seen a war movie?" I asked. The majority were shaking their heads yes. "Do you remember seeing a priest giving last rites to a dying man on some beachhead or in a foxhole?"

"I have," Rob replied.

"Somebody has to provide covering fire and protect them. They make sure their Marines and Sailors find their way to their final destination in life. But don't think these cats are anything less than the men and women they serve. They're not. I am sure nine Medals of Honor have been awarded to chaplains, usually posthumously. If you boys learn anything from me, there is nothing funny about being dead. The few I have known; I would have followed them anywhere! They are true warriors, and they are not all they seem. Some had past lives prior to finding God, and some are as good a death dealers as any of these heartbreaker and life takers you see here."

"Interesting. Maybe I will come back to that later. I'll make a note of that." He looks down and writes something on his big yellow notepad. Looking back at me, "So what about the padre and the preacher Jack was talking about?" John asked.

"He is talking about Commander Joseph Johnson and Lt (JG) Brian Stolley. They're the two Chaplains who deployed with most of us here last year to the Balkans in '96…". Before I could say anymore, Lance Corporal Frankie the Freak interpreted.

"Father Johnson is one steely-eyed man of God! He may be little, but that fireplug is strong as an ox and crazier than Staff Sergeant Hart's pet coon and most of Stanley's looney-ass girlfriends combined."

Stanley interrupts, "Hey, I am sitting right here!"

Looking over at Stanley, "And your point?" Frankie asks.

Stanley shrugs his shoulders.

"Exactly!" Frankie shouts.

Just loud enough to overpower the two of them, "At *ease*, you two! *Damn*, I swear it's like having two five-year-olds around with the two of you! Except for a couple of five-year-olds will listen to you, *sometimes*."

Lance Corporal Frankie stiffens up, "Sorry, HM2!" I started to shake my head yes to acknowledge it was ok, then I looked across the table.

Stanley looks me straight in the eye, as usual, "*Fine*! I'll just sit here and *drink* my drink."

"Sounds Like an amazing idea, Stanley." Turning back towards Rob and John, I continued, "Father Johnson is an anomaly. First, he is one of the smartest men I have known. I guess that goes along with being a Jesuit priest. Of course, it is a given he has given himself to God first, but his next calling is to service the hearts, minds, and eternal souls of men and women in uniform."

Stopping his intensive sketching to sharpen some of his pencils, Rob looks over at me, "Frank, what did Frankie mean when he called the Father a steely-eyed man of God?"

Kinda shocked, wondering what rock these two had been living under, "You ever heard the term *Steely-eyed Missile Man?*"

Shaking his head, "No, I don't think so. Where would I have heard it?"

A little shocked at his answer, "I am not sure of its true origin, maybe NASA, but *we*," holding my arms up in the air to mimic a hugging/holding gesture, "use it as a reference to someone who is willing to step up and step out of his comfort zone. A reference to an individual who is willing to place themselves in harm's way for the good of the mission, their country, their Corps, their unit, and most importantly – their brothers and sisters in arms. It's that guy or gal who weighs their own needs, goals, aspirations, etc., against the good of others and will always put the mission and/or the welfare of others above theirs. That's what a Steely-eyed Missile Man is."

Looking perplexed, John, in a voice that was more of a statement than a question, said, "I thought that's what priests were supposed to do."

"You're correct in theory," I said as I leaned back in my chair and swigged my Tequila Sunrise's last drink. "Creager, can you get me a Shiner in a bottle, please?" Creager nodded yes, as he gathered up the empties and headed toward the bar.

"You see, the chaplain is assigned to us, and they," using my hand to make air quotes, "are supposed to train with us. Go the field with us. Do all the miserable shit we do, but I have yet to run across a battalion commander who is willing to cross that line and *force* a man of the cloth to do what he really doesn't want to do. I think most think it's poor performance, and it's like that old belief from back home. I don't believe in ghosts, but I don't play in cemeteries after dark either if you know what I mean, Vern?" Most shook their heads in agreement.

"But Father Johnson, who in person everyone calls *Padre*, at least in our battalion, well, that's what I thought anyway. But a couple of weeks ago, I was over at BLDG 65 picking up some medical records, and I saw the CG, General Howell, talking to him, and he called him *Padre*...Thanks, Creager!" taking the beer Creager handed me.

"Back to the point, Father Johnson is always at morning PT with one of the companies and never misses Friday's battalion PT. Hell, on road marches, that little fire plug carries a large A.L.I.C.E pack! Even seen him hump an 81-mm mortar base plate a time or two. Most Marines only carry a medium ruck. If we're in the field, cold, wet, miserable (making sure to enunciate "we're"), the Padre is *cold*, *wet*, and *miserable too*! That is why the Marines and Sailors respect him so much! I don't see many TV preachers doing that."

Stanley putting in his two cents, "That base plate is no fucking joke! That damn thing weighs close to thirty fucking pounds!"

Never missing a chance to screw with Stanley, Lance Corporal Frankie perks up and interjects, "Actually, Doc, the M252 81mm Medium Crew Served Mortar's base plate - the M3A1 base plate, to be precise weighs twenty-nine pounds or thirteen kilograms for any *Limey's*, excuse me, allied partners from across the pond among us, which I do not believe we have any here tonight."

Stanley turns to Lance Corporal Frankie, giving him the two-hand bird salute, "Like I said, *close to thirty fucking pounds!*"

"Do you two ever stop?" Shaking my head, I turn back toward Rob and John.

Raising his eyebrows in interest, causing his forehead to wrinkle, John spoke up, "Gotta agree with you there, Frank! About him not being a *TV preacher.* So, what about this preacher? Is he the same caliber of a leader?" Smirking, he asked, "Is he cut from the same cloth, so to speak?"

"Not even close. Calling Father Johnson *Padre* is truly a term of endearment. The *Preacher,* on the other hand, is anything but! Father Johnson wears the title of Padre with pride, like a badge of honor. Lieutenant (JG) Stolley, on the other hand, I am pretty sure despises with every ounce of his being called *Preacher* and will till the day God calls him home."

Rob looked up from his drawing, "I can see why a priest would resent being called a preacher. Seems condescending."

"I agree with you one hundred percent if he was a priest, but he's a bonafide, card-carrying, Southern Baptist preacher. Graduated from Campbell University, School of Divinity in Buies

Creek, North Carolina," I said. "It's not so much that the guys call him Preacher, but rather how he got the name."

"Father Johnson, he is truly one of us. Lieutenant Stolley, not so much. I think he is here because he believes that we," leaning back while stretching my arms wide, "Marines and Sailors, probably anyone in uniform, are heathens! Our eternal souls are damned, and we are going straight to hell! Because of this, he has made it his personal mission to save us all from ourselves before it's too late."

With a look of complete bewilderment, Rob first looks around the table, at John, then at me. "Why does he think you guys are so evil? I remember my dad talking about when he came home from Vietnam when people called him a baby killer. Still, I have never heard anyone describe today's military in such a derogatory manner."

"Hell, Dawg," pushing his chair back, Lance Corporal Frankie stood up and grabbed his empty bottles, "Killing is what Marines were put on earth by God to do! It is our divine mission in life! Haven't you ever watched *Full Metal Jacket*? Besides, it's the first line in our job description - Join the Corps, travel to far away, distant and exotic places, meet interesting people, and kill all the bad motherfuckers there!" He looked at me, "You know how it is, Doc. '*Operators gotta Operate*!' Anybody needs anything?"

You can't help but smile, "I am good, but looks like John and Rob could use another round," I reply.

"On it, Doc," Lance Corporal Frankie replies as he turns and heads towards the bar, followed by Stanley, Gilpen, and Creager.

Trying to gauge Lance Corporal Frankie's response, John asks me, "Does he really believe that...."

"That macho bullshit?" I interject.

"Yes, that."

To emphasize my point, I slowly enunciate, "Every single word of it!" I started shaking my head and laughing as I finished. "You've heard the term *drink the Kool-Aid*, right?"

Acknowledging my question, Rob said, "Yeah, it is basically a dig on someone or a group of people with a cult-like belief in something or belief system. Giving some shit for blindly accepting or buying into something without thinking, researching, questioning, or criticizing. Didn't it originally refer to a cult down in South America who drank Kool-Aid laced with cyanide to kill themselves?"

"Exactly, The Reverend Jim Jones and the Peoples Temple of the Disciples of Christ. He was a real whack-job, no doubt there! He may have made the term *drink the Kool-Aid* common vernacular, but I promise you Marines have been indoctrinating recruits since 1775, two hundred years before Jim Jones was even a wet stain on his mom's sheets! He was an egomaniac with no purpose other than getting his own jollies off. Marines believe they have a divine purpose, hence the need for chaplains."

Questioning my reasoning, Rob asked, "So if they are so divine, why does Lieutenant Stolley believe you are all damned and he has to save your soul?"

From behind me, "That easy." HM3 Gilpen sat a couple of fresh pints of Shiner down in front of Rob and John, "Alcohol!"

Dumbfounded, Rob replied, "Alcohol?"

Taking his seat, Gilpen continues, "It's the Devil's elixir! According to the Preacher, anyway! Don't believe me, come by the barracks on Sunday morning around 0700. He'll be out front preaching to anyone who will listen. Says drinking alcohol only leads to sin, and sin leads to hell! Says we have to repent!"

"Really, that's fucking messed up! Is that why you guys call him The Preacher?" John asked.

Jumping back into the conversation, "No, that's what most people think, but it's not the reason. It stems back to the Fall of '96. Many of us here served with Battalion Landing Team 2/8 (BLT 2/8), part of the 24th Marine Expeditionary Unit - Special Operations Capable (MEU-SOC), on the USS Saipan (LHA-2) on a Med Cruise in the Adriatic Sea. We spent a month or more doing gator squares off the coast of Croatia in support of Operation Decisive Endeavor. The Padre was the BLT Chaplain, and the Preacher and the MEU's chaplain both resided with us on the Saipan."

"Gator Navy Baby!" Stanley broadcasted like a heckler from the cheap seats.

"The Gator Navy? I didn't understand your reference to Gator Squares, either." Rob said, stopping a minute from sketching his next Van Gogh.

"Sorry, guys. The Gator Navy, it's all the ships and its accompaniments that comprise the Navy's amphibious assault ships." I explained.

With both hands in the air giving the Shaka sign, Lance Corporal Frankie interjects, "The big, grey taxi service for Marines." He started laughing, quite pleased with himself and his interservice rivalry jab.

"Frankie, you know what MARINE stands for, right?" By the half-smile on his face, he knew my answer. I just could not help myself; he opened that door! With an enigmatic smile, I replied, "**M**y **A**ss **R**ides **I**n **N**avy **E**quipment!"

"Reeling it back in here," trying to get back to my original story, "we finally had a Port of Call in Trieste, Italy, after doing thirty-plus days of gator squares in the Adriatic. Have you ever been to Trieste?" I asked.

John said, "The only place I've ever been outside of the country was when we went to Cancun on my senior trip. Rob, what about you?"

"Rob shook his head no." I took it he'd never left the CONUS. "Trieste is one of the major deepwater port cities on the very northeast end of the Adriatic Sea. It's a narrow strip of land that Slovenia borders to the east and 19 miles north of Croatia. We were there for four days. I pulled Shore Patrol the night before with Gilpen and Stanley. I needed something sustainable other than galley food and some European beer." I paused to take a big swig of my beer, finishing it off.

"Gilpen and I headed out on the town. We were late getting off the ship. Gilpen had gotten food poisoning, or some shit the night before and was vomiting his ass off, so I threw in a couple of 18 gauge IVs on him and tanked him up with fluids and a gram of Rocephin which should have killed anything incubating in him. We were not missing out on Liberty."

Across the table, Gilpen just shrugged his shoulders and smirked. "Like Frankie says, *Operators Gotta Operate.*"

Picking back up where I had left off, "We were walking down the Viale XX Settembre, it's a beautiful tree-lined street with many bars and restaurants. Gilpen spotted the Padre in a little outside bar, sitting by himself. The Padre was, is always, good for a round or two. The man loves to drink his beer, which really puts him at odds with Lieutenant. Stolley."

Rob politely interrupted, "Sorry, I still don't get it. Why does drinking beer put him at odds with Lieutenant Stolley? I am Catholic myself. I've never seen drinking being frowned upon by the clergy."

"HM2. Care if I answer that?" Stanley asked.

"Go ahead, Tobey."

Stanley provided his explanation, "Rob, it's like my dad used to say - *'You never* take a Baptist fishing, *you always* take two. If you take just one, he'll drink all your beer. If you take two, they're both so worried the other will tell each other, they won't drink a drop.' He also said, 'At least when you see a Catholic in the liquor store, he'll acknowledge you and stop and talk!' Oh, and if the Baptist had helped support the local liquor store instead of the one in the next county over because they were so afraid of someone seeing them, Jim could have kept the local liquor store afloat!"

Rob leaned back and looked up, "I think I am starting to get the picture now."

"Gilpen and I walked over. He asked us to sit down. As I said earlier, the Padre is one of the wisest men I have ever known! He started talking about the history of the city. He was rambling about how during the Crusades; it had been one of the port cities of the Republic of Venice. He talked about how Venice had built ships for Pope Innocent III's calls for a Fourth Crusade. That led him into a lengthy exposition on the Crusades, which was cool since we were headed to Turkey and Israel next. We were three,, maybe four, hell, maybe more rounds deep, and the group had grown by ten-to-fifteen. A few Corpsmen, Lance Corporal Frankie, Staff Sergeant Hart, Gunney Hall, and his crew, and some others when Lieutenant Stolley appeared out of nowhere."

His contempt for us was not masked as he attempted to intimidate the Padre with a wide stance and slightly tucked chin, "Sir, can I speak to you...privately?"

"Is there a problem, Lieutenant?" the Padre asked.

"Sir, I just think we need to speak privately. About..."

"About what, Lieutenant? Is there a problem with one of us? Why don't you have a seat, and we can discuss it," the Padre said as he pulled the empty chair to his immediate right out from the table in an offer for the Lieutenant to join us.

The Lieutenant put his hands on his hips, "Sir, I think what you are doing here with the men is inappropriate behavior for clergy."

The Padre raised one eyebrow, straightened his shoulders, and sat up in his chair, "Lieutenant, I think you need to be a little more *specific* on what you mean by *inappropriate behavior for clergy.*"

Head lifted, chest pushed out, Lieutenant Stolley proclaimed, "Sir, Ephesians 5:18 states thou shall not be drunk with wine!"

Leaning forward, both forearms resting on the table, slowly taking a deep breath. Just as slow, the Padre exhaled. You could see he was trying to control his response. His eye contact never wavered. "Actually, Lieutenant Stolley, in your King James Version of the Bible, Ephesians 5:18 says, *And be not drunk with wine, wherein is excess; but be filled with the Spirit.* Regardless, I know! It's not your point. But to your point, Preacher, we are not drinking wine. We are drinking beer, so either belly up or shut up. I don't care which!"

Raising his hand to his mouth, "Damn, that's some harsh shit, dude! What did the Lieutenant just do? Rob asked.

"At first, he just stood there, wide-eyed, mouth open, then his face flushed, his ears turned fire engine red, he kept opening his fingers wide, then clenching his fist tight! He turned and walked off, never saying another word." I paused for a moment to take a drink.

"We had a couple more rounds, then we all returned to the ship. If you get my drift, the Padre needed some navigational aid returning to port. We cross the Quarter Deck and help him up to O-country. But the next day, the Preacher's name was sealed." Rob was looking up, curious. John was tuned in, as well as the others.

"Every day before Liberty, the BLT would assemble on the flight deck for the daily liberty brief. The CO or XO had some moto bullshit speech, and the sergeant major threatened us with the consequences of us fucking up. After it was over, the medical staff from the BLT, MEU, and ship assembled in the hangar deck, and the clergy joined us as well. We were hashing out the daily medical brief about the medical evac plan in case of a mass casualty event. The MEU CO, Col Numb Nuts, walked up to listen in on our plan. When we were done, he turned and walked away. As he strolled toward the passageway, he passed Father Johnson and Lieutenant Stolley, and we heard him address them.

"Good morning, Padre! Good to see you, Preacher Stolley."

"We lost our shit! We started laughing. We couldn't fucking help it! He was pissed! There were daggers in his eye that morning! Pretty sure he damned us all to hell! Anyway, since that day, he has been known as Preacher Stolley. He is a full Lieutenant now. That fella's, is the story of the Padre and the Preacher."

John tilted his head back, "That's crazy, Frank. Thanks for sharing."

Pushing my chair back, "My pleasure, but you are going to have to excuse me. It looks like my steak is getting cold over there! I am sure these boys have plenty more Sea Stories for you..."

Closing Time, You Don't Have to Go Home... Just Remember Bad Decisions Make Good Stories

0145
Saturday
Jack's BAS Bar & Grill
Hwy 17
Jacksonville, NC

Ding, *Ding, Ding, Ding* rang out from the ship's bell behind the bar. Everything stopped, and it became the quietest it had been since we got here around 1600 earlier, well, I guess, yesterday now.

Standing behind the register, "All ashore who's going ashore," Senior yelled. "You don't have to go home, however, folks, the State of North Carolina ABC Commission says you can't stay here. Please tab out before you leave. Please don't make me send Little Joe after you. You know how cranky he can be! Bad decisions make great stories, but not while you're looking through bars wearing shiny bracelets. Remember that! Don't drive if you've been drinking. Take the free ride."

By this time, most had already left. Phillips stuck to his one beer rule and headed south on 17, blaring "Radar Love" as he left the parking lot. That hunter green Electra Glide was beautiful. Hopefully, John's bike will be fixed tomorrow. If not, I might still ride with him towards Topsail Island for an hour or two while John bangs out some words. Creager had loaded Stanley up and was headed back towards the barracks. Smitty had an ambulance full of patients and was headed that way as well. I have to say that the limo service is a pretty cool idea! HM2 Sox had left with Staff Sergeant Hart and his wife around midnight but looks like Frankie the Freak has scored. Frankie and Tiff's friend Amanda have hit it off. She's been hanging in his back pocket pretty close since she got here around midnight. They're still playing pool in the back.

The last two days have been eye-opening for me. I was in a fraternity in college, and we like to say we are brothers who will do anything for each other, but compared to these guys, we are nothing but a bunch of pretenders. These guys are the real deal. As I heard Staff Sergeant Hart say, they are tight, watertight as a frog's ass. Their bond is hard to describe. They are closer than a family. They are their own tribe, with their own language. If you have never lived a life, you will never understand it and likely never believe the stories they tell. Senior was right. There is more than one book's worth of material here. Going through my sketches, I think we have enough from just tonight for the first book.

John made his way back from smoking outside, followed by Frankie and Amanda.

"Hey, Frankie. You got a couple of minutes to answer a few questions for me?" I asked as he and Amanda were walking past.

"Sure, my man, what up?" he replied.

"You seem to be close with these guys, like Three Musketeers, all-for-one, and one-for-all," I said, trying to get my thoughts across and out of my head without sounding like a real dumbass.

"Brothers from different mothers. I would be pushing up daisies if it were not for these guys. Why do you ask?" Frankie asked me, with a puzzled look on his face.

"Just an outsider looking in, trying to make sure we, I mean – I, get it right in my drawings," I replied.

"What's there to get right? Draw what you hear and see." Frankie said, "These guys ain't difficult to understand."

"What I hear is these guys bashing on Marines all night, making fun of you guys, and you giving it back just as hard, of course. I guess there is some part of me that... I don't," I said, stammering trying to find the right words.

Understanding what I was getting at, Frankie found the words for me. "What? You don't get the bond between Corpsmen and Marines?"

"Exactly!" I said.

Looking around at Amanda, then back towards John and me, Frankie started to explain, "There was a Marine general. I don't remember his name or when he said it, but he was asked to describe a Navy Corpsman, most likely to some newspaper reporter. If you want a word for word, I am sure you can find the who, what, when, and where somewhere, but the gist was this - A FMF Navy Corpsman is a long haired, in dire need of a fresh shave, mustache always out of regs, lost his military bearing, slept in uniform wearing, Hershey bar boot shining, Marine-hatin' Sailor with specific medical skills, who will go through the very gates of

Hell to get to a wounded Marine. That, my young Padawan, is the very essence of who these men and women are!"

John jumped into the conversation, "You truly love these guys, don't you, Frankie!"

"Brother, I was not joking when I said I would be pushing up daisies if it wasn't for these guys. It wasn't a figure of speech. I owe my life to Stanley. One night down in Panama, our RAC, which is a river patrol boat, was hit by a drug-running boat, and I was thrown overboard. Somehow, I hit my head on the side of the boat and was out cold like dead fish on ice. That crazy bastard jumped in the water with all his damn gear on, dove down, and pulled me to the surface. I would have drowned in the Canal if it weren't for him."

After processing what I heard, "That's some stoic hero shit right there!" I said.

"I know, right," Frankie said. "All you have to do is sit and listen. These guys are the real deal, but the stupid shit they do. That is what will sell books. Everyone already writes about the hero stuff. Libraries are full of that. Nobody writes about the stuff that makes you scratch your head going, 'What the fuck?' That just didn't really happen, did it?"

"Well, we're here for several more days! We've got enough material for a couple of books already. Can't wait to see what tomorrow holds!" I said.

"Boys, Senior is walking this way. He's about to kick our asses to the curb. We'll see you tomorrow?" Frankie said, and he and Amanda started making their way to the door.

I sat down and started going through my drawing. I wonder where this is going to take us.

"John, you ready to head out?" I asked.

"Yeah, let's get out of here. I am beat!" he said.

"Hey, Senior, we are headed out. We'll see you…"

Till next time, my friends!

We will see you in the –

- *Tales from the Green Side Volume #2*
- *Tales from the Back of the Buse Volume #1*
- *Tales from the ER Volume #1*

About the Author and Illustrator

<u>Johnnie L Gilpen Jr PA-C CAQ(EM) NRP</u>

Johnnie is a former US Navy 8404 FMF Hospital Corpsman. Johnnie served with the 2nd Battalion, 8th Marines, 2nd Marine Division, and deployed with the 24th Marine Expeditionary Unit (MEU-SOC). Johnnie currently works as a pediatric emergency medicine physician assistant at the OU Health Children's Hospital. He says, "Taking care of kids is like taking care of Marines, except the kids don't cry as much or eat as many crayons! They have the same mentality - they don't know they're supposed to be hurt. They just brush it off and keep going!" Johnnie enjoys hiking, fishing, boating, kayaking, and camping with his wife, Leslie, and their dogs, Cookie, Harley, and Cooper. They live in Union City, Oklahoma, but love to travel. Johnnie and Rob served together in the Navy and have maintained their friendship over the last 25-plus years, taking family vacations together to the Florida Keys as often as possible, as well as teaching first responders around the country together.

Robert Creager FF/NRP

Robert "Bob" Creager born in Ponce, Puerto Rico is a retired Lieutenant with over 25 years of service as a Firefighter, Paramedic, and Tactical Medic. Bob is a former U.S. Navy 8404 Hospital Corpsman who served 12 years with the Fleet Marine Force (FMF). Bob served as a platoon corpsman with Weapons Company, 2nd Battalion, 2nd Marines, and 3rd Force Reconnaissance Company. He currently works as an EMS and rescue training Captain with the Reedy Creek Fire Department in Orlando, Florida. Bob currently lives in Florida with his wife Malinda, daughter Taylor, son Robbie, and their dog. You can find him on the ocean when he is not teaching or working.

Author Contact Information

Booking requests please reach out to one of the following:

Email: info@johnniegilpen.com

Mailing address: 8404 Publishing LLC
7997 Alfadale Street
Union City, Oklahoma 73090

Phone: (405) 633 – 1190

info@johnniegilpen.com
(405) 633 - 1190

Learn more at: https://www.amazon.com/author/johnniegilpen

Publisher Contact Information

For information regarding publishing please reach out to one of the following

Email: info@8404publishing.com

Mailing address: 8404 Publishing LLC
7997 Alfadale Street
Union City, Oklahoma 73090

8404

Publishing LLC
www.8404publishing.com

The Barstool Dictionary

<u>A – (Alpha)</u>

ABC's: Airway, Breathing, & Circulation

Aft: Naval terminology – *aft* is the inside (onboard) rearmost part of the vessel, while stern refers to the outside (offboard) rearmost part of the vessel.

A.L.I.C.E: All-purpose Lightweight Individual Carrying Equipment

AO: Area of Operation

At ease: In the military - in a relaxed attitude with the feet apart and the hands behind the back.

<u>B – (Bravo)</u>

BAS: Battalion Aid Station

BLT: Battalion Landing Team

Blue Water Navy: Navy assigned to naval ships at sea.

Boot: Derogatory term to describe a new military, police, EMS, or fire service member.

Bus: EMS slang for an ambulance

Butts: Slang for cigarette butts

C – (Charlie)

CCU: Corrective Custodial Unit

CG: Commanding General

CO: Commanding Officer

Colorado Kool-Aid: Slang term for Coors Banquet Beer

CONUS: Continental United States

Corporal (Cpl): USMC & USA (E-4)

D –(Delta)

DD: Designated Driver

DRT: Dead Right There

Doughboys: Popular nickname for the American infantryman during World War I.

DOB: Date of birth

Drink the Kool-Aid: To accept or buy into something blindly without thinking, researching, questioning, or criticizing. A dig on someone or a group of people that have a cult-like belief in something or belief system. Originated from the Jonestown Massacre, where people drank cyanide-laced Kool-Aid.

E – (Echo)

EGA: Eagle, Globe, and Anchor – the U.S. Marine Corps emblem.

EMS: Emergency Medical Services

ETA: Estimated Time of Arrival

F – (Foxtrot)

FMF (Fleet Marine Force): In the Navy, it refers to naval personnel assigned to Marine units.

FOD: Foreign Object Debris

FSSG: Field Service Support Group

G – (Golf)

G.I. Joe: Refers to an enlisted soldier(s) in the US Army; Originated in WWII; often a slang term referring to enlisted personnel of any branch. G.I. is short for government issue.

GMO: General Medical Officer

Green Side: Navy/Marine Corps slang terminology referring to Navy personnel assigned to Marine units.

Gunwale: The top edge of a ship or boat

Gunnery Sgt: USMC (E-7)

Gunney: Slang for Gunnery Sergeant

Gunwale: Naval terminology – the *upper edge* of the side of a boat or ship.

H – (Hotel)

HA: Hospitalman Apprentice: USN (E-2)

HCG: Laboratory test to check for the level of Human Chorionic Gonadotropin – a pregnancy test.

Head: Naval term for bathroom

HN: Hospitalman; USN (E-3)

HQBN: Headquarters Battalion

HR: Hospitalman Recruit: USN (E-1)

I – (India)

J – (Juliet)

Joes: See G.I. Joe

Johnny Cash's: Slang Term refers to the black men's long-sleeved winter working uniform.

K – (Kilo)

KIA: Killed In Action

KISS: Keep It Simple Son (Stupid)

L – (Lima)

Lance Corporal (LCpl): USMC (E-3)

Legs: Slang used by Airborne-qualified service members to describe those who are not.

Lieutenant (JG): USN Lieutenant Junior Grade (O-2)

LHA: Landing Helicopter Assault - USN hull classification symbol for general purpose helicopter carrying amphibious assault ship. There are two classes - Tarawa and America.

Limey: American military slang for the British military. The term was originally derived from their use of limes to treat scurvy and the lack of understanding by American sailors.

LPH: Landing Platform Helicopter - USN hull classification symbol for general purpose helicopter carrying amphibious assault ship. There are currently no ships in the US Navy with this designation. The USS Iwo Jima was decommissioned in 2003.

M – (Mike)

Main Side: Description of the main part of the Camp Lejeune base.

MARDIV: Marine Division

Marine Regs: Refers to US Navy personnel assigned to FMF units who have opted to wear Marine regulation Class A, B, and C uniforms.

MAU: Marine Amphibious Unit

Med: Navy and Marine Corps slang for the Mediterranean area.

MEF: Marine Expeditionary Force

MEU-SOC: Marine Expeditionary Unit - Special Operations Capable

MIA: Missing In Action

Mike's: Military/Law Enforcement/ EMS/ FIRE slang for minutes or meters depending on the conversation and reference.

MOS: Military Occupation Specialty

MWR: Moral, Welfare, and Recreation

N – (November)

Navy-Marine Corps Medal: The highest non-combat decoration awarded for heroism by the United States Department of the Navy to members of the United States Navy and United States Marine Corps. The medal was established by an act of Congress on 7 August 1942, and is authorized under 10 U.S.C. § 6246. It is the equivalent of the Army's Soldier's Medal, Air and Space Forces' Airman's Medal, and the Coast Guard Medal.

NEC: Navy enlisted manpower and personnel classifications.

NCO: Non-commissioned Officer

O – (Oscar)

OCONUS: Outside of the Continental United States

OOD: Officer of the Day

P – (Papa)

PA: Physician Assistant/Associate (PA-C)

PFC: Private First Class: USMC (E-2); USA (E-3)

Phrogs: Marine slang for a CH-46 Sea Knight helicopter.

Port: Naval terminology – *left* side of a ship or boat

POV: Privately Owned Vehicle

PT: Physical Training

Q – (Quebec)

R – (Romeo)

RAC: Riverine Assault Craft

S – (Siera)

Scuttlebutt: Navy slang for gossip or rumor

Sergeant (Sgt): USMC & USA (E-5)

Staff Sergeant (SSgt) or Staff Sgt: USMC & USA   (E-6)

Starboard:　Naval terminology – *right* side of a ship or boat.

Stern:　Naval terminology – aft is the inside (onboard) rearmost part of the vessel, while *stern* refers to the outside (offboard) rearmost part of the vessel.

Squid:　Derogatory slang to describe Navy personnel.

T – (Tango)

Tin Can:　WWII Navy slang term for a Destroyer

U – (Uniform)

V – (Victor)

W – (Whiskey)

Water bull:　Potable (drinking) water tank usually several hundred gallons in size, often a self-contained, towable trailer

Winger: Marine slang term for a Marine assigned to the Marine Air Wing

WM: Slang for a female Marine - Women Marine

X – (X-ray)

XO: Executive Officer; Second Officer in command

Y – (Yankee)

Yellow Jackets: Slang term for Coors Banquet Beer

Z – (Zulu)

Military Occupational Specialty (MOS)

U.S. Army

11B – Infantryman MOS: The infantryman supervises, leads, or serves as a member of an infantry activity that employs individual small arms weapons or heavy anti-armor crew served weapons, either vehicle or dismounted in support of offensive and defensive combat operations.[5]

18D – Special Forces Medical Sergeant: Ensures detachment medical readiness prior to deployment; orders, stores, and distributes medical and dental supplies, equipment, and medicine; performs medical evaluation and care and treatment of allied and indigenous personnel; operates combat laboratory and treats emergency and trauma patients; arranges and facilitates medical evacuations; provides care to team members and establishes temporary medical facilities to support operations; diagnoses and treats medical conditions

---

[5] https://www.cool.osd.mil/army/moc/index.html?moc=11b&tab=mocselect

with appropriate medications; collects and disseminates medical intelligence.[6]

---

[6] https://www.armywriter.com/NCOER/18D.htm

U.S. Marine Corps

0311 – Infantry Rifleman: The Riflemen employ the M16M4/A4 Service Rifle, the M203 Grenade Launcher and the M27 Infantry Automatic Rifle (IAR). Riflemen are the primary scouts, assault, and close combat forces available to the MAGTF. They are the foundation of the Marine Infantry Organization, and as such are the nucleus of the fire team in the rifle squad, the scout team in the LAR Squad, and Scout Snipers in the infantry battalion. Noncommissioned Officers are assigned as Fire Team Leaders, Scout Team Leaders, and Rifle Squad Leaders.[7]

0331 – Machine Gunner: The Machine Gunner is responsible for the tactical employment of the 7.62 mm Medium Machine-Gun, the 50 cal., and 40mm Heavy Machine-Gun, and their support vehicle. Machine Gunners provide direct fire in support of the Infantry Rifle squads/platoons/companies. They are located in the weapons platoons of the rifle and weapons company in the infantry battalion. Noncommissioned Officers are assigned as team leaders and squad leaders/section leaders.[8]

---

[7] https://www.cool.osd.mil/usmc/moc/index.html?moc=0311&tab=overview
[8] https://www.cool.osd.mil/usmc/moc/index.html?moc=0331&tab=overview

U.S. Navy

Hospital Corpsman (HM) (0000): duties and responsibilities to maintain patient treatment records, conduct research and perform clinical tests. Assist Navy Physicians and Nurses in a variety of medical fields, including, but not limited to: radiology, physical therapy, phlebotomy, dental, surgery, family medicine, pathology, women's health and more.

Hospital Corpsman (HM) Field Service Medical Technician (8404): Field Medical Service Technicians provide medical services to various commands of the Navy and Marine Corps in a worldwide operational environment. Conduct technical and administrative medical assistance supporting the mission and functions of field units. Maintain field treatment facilities rendering routine medical and emergency care to unit personnel and combatants. Coordinate and perform medical and casualty evacuation procedures. Ensure the observance of field sanitary and preventive medicine measures supporting force health protection. Assist with the procurement and distribution of related supplies and equipment for peacetime use and in combat areas. Conduct health and medical education training programs. FMF Dental Technicians assist Dental Officers in providing dental treatment in the field. Provide technical and administrative assistance to support the mission and functions of Navy and Marine Corps field units. Assist with the procurement and distribution of related supplies and equipment for peacetime use and in combat areas. Augment and assist medical personnel in providing emergency medical care to field or combat casualties, field sanitary measures, and medical/casualty evacuation procedures. Conduct health and dental education training programs supporting force health protection.[9]

[9] https://www.cool.osd.mil/usn/moc/index.html?moc=hm_fmf_mt&tab=overview

Coming in the future...

Two Minutes:

A Walt Claborn Novel

Prologue

10:37 October 24th, 2015
Latitude Longitude
Washington D.C.

"Do you know the difference between a war story and a fairy tale?" I replied as Dennis sat next to me, shaking his head, mumbling something to himself.

"No, please enlighten us!" echoed down from the man who was sitting in front of us.

"A fairy tale usually starts with once upon a time…," then interrupting me with what I felt was a very condescending tone.

"And a war story usually starts with there I was… and at some point, the conversation includes really guys, you can't make this shit up. Am I correct?"

Here we are again! Hell, here I am again! How? Why does this shit keep happening to me? You think that we would learn. Hell, you think I would learn!

Keeping my cool, I slowly looked around the room. I took a deep breath, "Really, Senator, that's how it happened! Honest injun!"

With a scowl on his face, turning towards Dennis with what I am sure he thought was an icy stare, "Do you have anything to add, Mr. Halcome?"

Snapping to attention in his seat, with his normal, satirical, South Brooklyn accent, "Your Honor, you forgot the part about hold my beer and watch this shit...... and sir... Orange is really not my best color, it makes my ass look big".

"God Damn it! Do you two realize how much trouble you're in?"

"Sir, yes, Sir!" we replied in unison.

"My gut tells me to bury you two misfits under Leavenworth and lock the rest of that motley crew of yours in the deepest, darkest hole I can find and forget where it is!"

"Director Burden, you and your band of merry men do not seem to understand that this is a Congressional hearing regarding their actions. Better yet, your actions or lack thereof over the last three months? All three of you seem to have forgotten you are under oath? Your demeanor, and your answers to our questions, specifically, my questions are disrespectful..." blah, blah, blah, yeah, yeah, yeah.

I always wanted to be Jack Bauer, but this is taking it a little too far...

PART ONE: The Picture is Fuzzy

Chapter One – Man in the Mirror

05:13 May 9th, 2015

Latitude: 24°34'10.62"N, Longitude: -81°45'10.98" W

Days Inn Motel

Key West, FL

I heard somewhere that Zoë Castillio[10] said "Every story has a beginning and an end, but sometimes they are one and the same".

Do not ask me who in the hell Zoë Castillio is, but for me, it rings too true for comfort. Standing here, staring at a reflection of a man I no longer recognize… Where did all this gray come from? The hollowness in my eyes. My face bares the lines and scars of more miles than I can remember. Damn sure more than I want too!

"Damn, it hurts to breathe!" Holding my side, staring at my reflection. I keep asking myself, *When do you call it quits, hang it all up?*

---

[10] Zoe Castillio. (2006). Dreamfall: The longest journey

The tattoos on my arms have begun to fade. The EGA, a reminder of a life, long past. The caduceus of who I once was… The helmet, rifle, bayonet, and combat boots and the 14 names etched on my side, a permanent reminder of those who did not come home. A permanent memorial. A promise to never forget. Twenty years, and the ghosts of my past still haunt me. Most days they come like an old black and white home movie. Others, like a Hollywood horror film. Today, they are weighing heavy on my soul… Twenty years ago today, I lost them. Twenty years ago, a piece of my soul was ripped from body…

Today is my birthday. My driver license says I am 48, the reflection in the mirror twice that.

Where do I start?

Chapter Two – My Brothers

Old men forget; yet all shall be forgot
But he'll remember with advantages
What feats he did that day. Then shall our names,
Familiar in his mouth as household words,
Harry the King, Bedford and Exeter,
Warwick and Talbot, Salisbury and Gloucester,
Be in their flowing cups freshly remembered.
This story shall the good man teach his son,
And Crispin Crispian shall ne'er go by,
From this day to the ending of the world,
But we in shall be rememberèd-
We few, we happy few, we band of brothers;
For he today that sheds his blood with me
Shall be my brother; be he ne'er so vile,
This day shall gentle his condition;
And gentleman in England now abed
Shall think themselves accursed they were not here,
And hold their manhoods cheap whiles any speaks
That fought with us upon Saint Crispin's day.

William Shakespeare – Henry V, Act 4 Scene 3, Page 3

06:45 May 10th, 1995
Latitude: 43°10'0.4938" N, Longitude: 17°12'36.4314" E
North of Drvenik, Croatia

"Doc, Cigarette?"

I looked up, Sgt. Bradford was looking down at me, a pack of Marlboros in his hand. I guess the smoking lamp is lit. *'Smokem' if you've gottem'*... I took one. Taking a knee beside me. He flipped open his zippo. The yellowish red flame flickered in the offshore breeze. With a long slow drag, the red fire moved rapidly through the tobacco, pulling the smoke into my lungs. I began to violently cough. A mouth full of phlegm came up. I tried to spit it out on the ground, but it was sticky and just hung from the corner of my mouth. It was black! Black from the burning fuel. Black from the smoldering frame that once was a magnificent chariot of war. As I sit over half a mile away, I can smell the burning JP-5. I still have the remnants, the lingering smell of flesh burning in my nostrils. Looking across the clearing, I can see the waves break as they come ashore. I can hear the sound of them crashing upon the rocks. In the distance can hear the Phrogs coming in. I close my eyes, I can see them, there not gone, they cannot be gone..........

LET ME KNOW WHAT YOU THINK

info@johnniegilpen.com
(405) 633 - 1190

www.ingramcontent.com/pod-product-compliance
Lightning Source LLC
Chambersburg PA
CBHW032004240626
47153CB00003B/1124